INTO THE EMBERS

BOOK FOUR OF THE LIGHT SERIES

JACQUELINE BROWN

Cover art designed by Aero Gallerie

Also by Jacqueline Brown
The Light, Book One of The Light Series
Through the Ashes, Book Two of The Light Series
From the Shadows, Book Three of The Light Series
Out of the Darkness, Book Five of The Light Series
"Before the Silence," a Light Series short story

To receive your FREE copy of "Before the Silence," please
visit www.Jacqueline-Brown.com.

This book is dedicated to all those who know, at the depth of their being, that love and sacrifice are intertwined.

One
BRIA

A blanket of mist covered our camp, filling the spaces between my sleeping friends with a damp haze. It would be hot today, as it had been the day before and the day before that. The nights cooled us off. The mixture of smoldering earth and chilled air created this low-hanging fog that brought with it a vividness of rebirth.

The moss covering the boulders that lined the winding creek was alive and green in the early morning dampness. My mind, too, was alert, though the night had been long, watching for threats that thankfully never came.

With Astrea beside me, even a raccoon would be detected; humans would be noticed long before they reached our camp. Especially humans in helicopters. The Lab alerted us to their approach at least thirty seconds before we could hear the first thump of the blades. Almost every day we found ourselves hiding under rocks or trees as the long, thin blades swirled overhead. There were more of them. It was difficult to tell how many—at least three, perhaps more. They were almost never directly overhead and were rarely going slow enough to see anyone. Still, they brought paralyzing fear with them. Each time, I worried this would be the time the commander found us. My friends would lie dead as the machine would lift me above the earth, taking me back to DC to pay for Trent's murder. I wondered about Blaise's parents. Would they be dead, with my friends, or flying above with the harvesters? I shook my head. These were not helpful thoughts. Besides, the helicopters were no longer hunting us.

The first few days after we escaped from the harvesters' camp were difficult. They did hunt us. We watched the helicopters dive low in the sky, as if they thought they'd found us. Thankfully, they never did.

On those days, we took turns carrying Astrea and splintered branches from trees and shrubs. We carried her because she couldn't walk, her leg broken by one of the harvesters when she'd saved my life. We carried the branches because they allowed us to cover ourselves better and faster. It worked. They never spotted us. Each day took us farther from the harvesters' camp. With each step, the paths we could take grew and the likelihood of their finding us decreased. They didn't know where we were going, that our home was in North Carolina, and that after being gone more than three months we were finally going home.

Now, as the helicopters flew higher and faster, we took comfort in the awareness that they weren't following us, merely expanding. Reclaiming a country they believed was theirs. With each helicopter came guilt. The guilt of leaving East and Haz to fight—without us. I told myself this fight was not mine. I reminded myself of the promise I had made to my father, that I would come home, that he would not lose another child. He needed me and Jonah's family needed him. With Sage pregnant, the argument was easier; she needed to be with our families to have her baby, to give her and her child a chance at surviving. And Juliette, too, was a reason to go home. This might be my fight, but it was definitely not hers. She deserved peace and she would find it there. We all would.

As I glanced at Blaise's parents, Richard and Felicia, I wondered if that was true. Would there be peace and safety with them around? They slept beside one another at the edge of our camp. It's where they always slept, beside one another and away from the rest of us. It was more than a week since we'd escaped from the harvesters. Since I had seen Richard and Felicia murder the young girl, Annalise, and her parents.

I wondered if the gruesome horror would ever fade enough for me not to remember it. I stared at them as they slept, the anger building inside me, causing my body to shake. I hated that they were with us. I didn't tell anyone else this, but it was the truth. I hated what they did. They had killed an innocent child and her parents. Their very existence disgusted me. How did they sleep? How did they function? How could anyone be so heartless and evil?

I turned away to slow the anger. It threatened, often, to overpower me. I turned back to them. They weren't evil. That's what made the killing so difficult. They weren't Trent.

They had been good. They had been good their entire lives. They cared about one another and their daughter and, by extension, about all of us. They were often kind and thoughtful. Helpful in all respects, and yet they had murdered.

We shared every meal and all supplies with them. But never had they offered an explanation. Or said they were sorry for their actions. They merely pretended the murders didn't happen or that they didn't matter. I couldn't understand this. I would never understand this and neither would Blaise.

She did all she could to avoid her parents, and when she was forced to interact with them, she did so with hatred. It oozed from her like pus demanding to be scraped clean. Perhaps it was time. Time to stop waiting for answers and demand them. We would be home soon—another few weeks—and then what? I would not lead killers to my dad or JP or any of the others. I would never allow that to happen. To have them around people I loved, people they could easily kill? No, I would not allow that.

Part of me wondered what the point was of even asking for an explanation. What could they say? Nearly all of us had killed someone. It was a grisly reality of our new world, so perhaps we had no right to judge. Killing to defend your own life was still killing, though in the case of self-defense, someone was going to die and you are choosing for that death

4

not to be your own. But when you shoot a child in the back after first killing her parents, that is murder.

It wasn't right for me to judge, but what they did was different than what the rest of us had done. It just was. Maybe they understood that, maybe they didn't. It didn't matter.

We had already made it through Pennsylvania and Maryland. Astrea's leg was almost healed, and still they said nothing. Only vague statements of the difficulty of living at the harvesters' camp. Of doing all they could to survive. Now that we were well into West Virginia, it seemed time for them to leave us. This world had changed them in a way I hoped it would never change me, and they could not go on with us. This was not me being judgmental; it was me being practical.

Sage mumbled as she slept. My gaze shifted to her. She was so beautiful, her face relaxed and peaceful. During the day it was different. Only Jonah and I knew her secret. Her belly remained flat and I supposed it would for several more weeks or, perhaps, months. She remained upbeat and happy around the others, joking and laughing freely. She never showed the pain of abandonment—unless she thought she was alone. During those times she allowed her smile to fade and her eyes to glaze over. Those times were coming more often. Her sister noticed them, but she thought they were because of the death of their mother. Yes, Faith's death was devastating for both Sara and Sage. But it was how they handled their mom's loss that defined them and their lives.

Sara turned inward, focusing even more on God. Her talks with Jonah were becoming more frequent and intense.

Sage had turned instead to Hayden. It was a mistake. The kind of mistake Sara and I had both made. A mistake that Sage would be forced to face for the rest of her life as their baby grew, first, within her, and then into a child and an adult. Would the baby have Hayden's eyes or his selfishness? Would he grow up to abandon the mother of his child? Would she grow into a woman who fell into the arms of any man that would have her? These were the questions Sage must be asking. And yet, from the outside, she seemed fine. A little sad, but nothing more.

Before the light, I had been like her—an actor playing a part. I wanted to blame it all on Trent, but that wasn't true. I had been pretending long before I met him and I would have kept on pretending. I was thankful in some strange way for the world falling away. Or not thankful, but appreciative of the good, at least in my life, that had come from such devastation.

I had shared that thought with Sara and she had said gratitude was a sign of spiritual awakening. I was sure I was not awakening, but I supposed I was at least vaguely curious about the things she and Jonah spoke of. So perhaps I was waking, though to what I had no idea.

Beside Sara, Juliette slept. She no longer cried out or whimpered in her sleep and her days were no longer silent.

She was most comfortable around Sara and when it was simply the two of them, Juliette dominated the conversation—so I was told. When the rest of us were there, Juliette spoke, but it was in a few whispered words.

Astrea lifted her head as Jonah awoke beside us. He stretched, his eyes blinking open. How beautiful he was in the gray morning light, or any light. His green eyes becoming alert, he sat up, combing his fingers through his tangled hair and pushing it behind his ears. His beard was thick. He said he was going to shave it off as soon as we got home, and I wasn't going to argue. Kissing him wasn't as fun with hair prickling my lips.

"Good morning," he said, reaching his arms around me, pulling me to him.

"Good morning," I whispered as I touched my lips to his.

"How was the night?" he asked, tucking strands of blonde hair behind my ears. The scar from Trent was almost completely covered.

"It was good. No sign of people. We heard some animals, but they stayed away."

He stretched. "That's good," he said, yawning.

I lay my body against his chest, feeling exhausted as I always did after a night watch.

"Sleep, at least until the others wake up and we break camp," he said, his arms around me, chasing the chill away.

I wanted to stay awake to have this time alone with him, but my eyes were already closing.

"For a minute," I mumbled, feeling his protective arms wrapped around me.

Two
EAST

Mom always said patience was not a virtue that came naturally to me, and so that meant I would need to try harder. I had always tried because she would want me to and I always, even from an early age, wanted to improve myself. But I was done trying. I was tired of sitting, tired of Seth's incessant whining, and tired of watching three people who we were either going to rescue or we weren't.

"We need to finish this," I said, crouching low, hiding in the shrubs that surrounded the expansive backyard of the President's retreat. "It's been three days. We've seen all we're going to see."

"I agree," Haz said. "Like I said, that guy—the older one—was a senator. The woman is familiar too, so she was probably a politician. The other one ...." He shrugged. "But they wouldn't have brought them to Camp David if there wasn't a reason. Which means there's a chance they can help us—"

"Save the world," Jael said, completing his thought with more than a hint of sarcasm.

She was right. It was crazy to think we could do anything to fix the way things were. But people change the world all the time. That's what Pops always told me. He was a good man and an amazing grandfather. I missed him every day and I doubted that would change, no matter how many days passed.

"The challenge is how to break them out and not be seen doing it," Ash said.

"That's impossible," Seth said, his voice like nails on a chalkboard.

I wished he had never come to our town. That was a mean thought, but it was true.

"Well," Jael snapped, "it's going to have to become possible, 'cause I'm not having them follow us home."

She had no parent until Mrs. Pryce took her in when she was twelve. Before that, she bounced from one lousy relative to another. She survived by seeing people for who they were. She didn't like Seth any more than I did. That realization brought me comfort. I didn't like not liking people, but if I was going to not like someone, it made me feel better that other people didn't like them too.

Seth had arrived at our town on the same day as Mr. and Mrs. Tait and their kids, but he showed up a few hours later. He said he had seen our fires and wanted to find out why there were so many. I was certain that was a lie. Jael and I agreed he had likely been following the Taits. After all, they had bags and a wagon full of supplies and only Mr. and Mrs. Tait could put up any real fight. Jael and I were sure Seth was preparing to ambush them. Only they made it to us first, so his plan was spoiled. The Taits were good people, loving and kind. As long as the town stood, they would not be hurt. That thought brought me peace. It was helpful in a moment like this, to remember why I was doing what I was doing.

When the Taits arrived, I was grateful. Not only because we could protect them and their kids, but because they told me of Jonah and the others. I was grateful they were not only alive but they were going in the correct direction. I shouldn't underestimate them, but without Haz and me, they were at a distinct disadvantage. It's why I volunteered to go with Sara and the others in the first place. Yes, I felt called to leave our home, but I also felt called to help them. If I hadn't gone and Jonah hadn't joined us, the other four wouldn't have survived past the first settlement at the river. Sara would've tried to ram the truck through a wall of people. Dozens of people would have been killed, including my friends. At that moment I understood why God had placed it in my heart to go with them. They needed me.

Since then, their survival skills had greatly increased. They would make it home. I believed that. If I didn't, I never would have stayed behind.

Seth clicked his teeth. The sound brought me back to the present and to my unending irritation with him.

"Are we going to stay here forever, then?" Seth said, his tone harsh. "There's no way to not be seen."

Jael and I exchanged a glance. I would risk my life breaking prisoners out so I could be away from him.

"Seth's right, in a totally negative downer sort of way," Ash said. "We can't stay here forever, and there are cameras all over that may or may not be working, and guards everywhere."

"Right. So let's take the prisoners and run. Fight our way out," Seth said. "We already made it through the fences. This is just an open yard."

"They weren't guarding the fences," Jael said. "All we had to do was crawl under them. There are half a dozen guards with weapons surrounding the prisoners at all times."

There was silence. None of us had known what to do for the last three days, but it was time to figure out a plan. We were out of food.

"After the pacing guy finishes pacing, he sits on that bench," Ash said. "What if we somehow left a note for him."

"Do you have paper?" Jael asked, her tone irritated.

"No," Ash answered, his expression falling in defeat.

"What if we threw rocks at him?" Seth said, grasping at nothing.

Haz raised an eyebrow, and I folded my arms.

I wished we hadn't let Seth come. I agreed to it only because I didn't trust him in town without us. As much as I disliked him here with me, I disliked the idea of him there, without me, even more.

Seth continued. "Not to hurt him, just to get his attention. If he saw us, I bet he'd figure out a way to communicate with us."

"You've had worse ideas," Ash said.

I studied the prisoner. He was pacing, as he almost always did. As I watched him, the memory of the first time I'd gone to the zoo entered my mind. I was six, we drove for hours, and as soon as we got there I wanted to leave. Seeing the animals in cages, their eyes so hollow and lonely, made me cry. I hated that zoo.

The pacing prisoner's eyes were wild with the pain of confinement and his skin was a sickly white and sunburned at the same time. His hair and beard were bushy and knotted and his clothes were rags. I wondered if Haz was right, that he had been, or still was someone important—like that lion at the zoo who had once been king of his jungle. Now the man was caged and, like the lion, he hated it. The path he walked was well worn as he paced around the wide yard. He wanted out more than the others. He was younger than the others too. Not as young as Haz, who was the oldest of our group, but no older than forty-five.

"Use this," Ash said, opening his pack. He pulled out a compact and handed it to Jael.

"Makeup?" she said.

"Yeah, your nose is shiny." He chuckled. "Naw, it's a mirror. Use it to signal him."

Trees blocked most of the sunlight, but Jael found a sliver. "We sure?" she asked.

Ash nodded. Haz pulled the pistol from his waistband. I did the same. Jael lifted her body subtly above the shrubs, finding a faint stream of light that poked through the leaves overhead. She angled the mirror, a beam of light hitting the man on the side of the face. He turned with a jerk, his abrupt movement alerting the guards. We crouched low, the shadows hiding us.

The man slapped at his face and then his leg, as if killing a bug. The guards relaxed. The man continued to pace along his path, shrewdly shifting his eyes toward us from time to time. The defeat in his eyes had been replaced by hope.

Three
BRIA

Richard stumbled, his foot sliding over a loose rock. The day was hot. Every day was hot. It was only at night, when the sun no longer beat down on us, that the temperature became comfortable.

"Are you okay?" Felicia asked him with concern.

"Fine," he answered, his voice tender.

Beside me, Blaise scoffed in anger. Her parents did not respond. Maybe they didn't hear her or maybe they understood she had every right to say whatever she felt. But she didn't. She kept it inside. She was seething with anger and she never said a word. Since she didn't say anything, the rest of us didn't think we had the right. But that wasn't true. We were leading murderers to the people that we loved. We had every right to try to understand—to make sure they weren't going to kill JP and Quinn while they slept or played.

I was staring at Felicia's hand in Richard's. How could they show one another, and all of us, kindness and yet so easily kill that family? How could they make those people into objects that were worthless, better dead, and yet value each other, and even us? I did not understand. I did not want to understand. I did not want them with us.

Jonah slipped his hand around mine, helping to shift my mind. Helping me focus less on Richard and Felicia and the murderers they were. Our hands became damp with sweat, but I didn't release Jonah's hand. It brought me peace and calm in a world that was anything but.

"Two more weeks," he had reminded me the night before. Two more weeks and we should be home. Two more weeks and I would be able to take a bath, with soap. We hadn't had soap since the shower at the gas station, when Hayden had been spying on us. We probably should have let Josh and Jonah beat him up. It would have saved Sage from all the pain he had caused her.

"Astrea needs to drink," Juliette whispered to Sara.

There was a winding stream to the left of us. We didn't walk close to it, though we kept near it.

"We'll stop for a few minutes," Sara said. "The rest will do us good."

She was right. The days were long. Sacrificing an hour during the middle of the heat allowed our bodies to cool and continue for longer than if we pushed all day.

As we neared the stream it felt as though air-conditioning had been turned on. I sat beside the stream, allowing my body to drape across the cool moss-covered stones that bordered the flowing water. Astrea stood with her paws in the water, lapping at the water. I watched with envy. If I drank straight from the stream I ran the risk of being sick for days. That was a risk none of us were prepared to take. Jonah filled first his bottle and then mine. I took the bottles from him and dropped in a few of the purification granules we'd stolen from the harvesters' camp. They were convenient, but tasted like chlorine. I preferred boiled water. However, we got that luxury only when we spent the night near water. I placed the cool bottle against my sweating neck as Jonah scooted beside me, our backs leaning against each other.

Blaise's parents sat by themselves, like they always did.

I felt Jonah's back straighten as he drew in a breath. "We need to talk," he said, his voice commanding, his long arms confidently pulled against his folded knees.

I sat up and turned to face him.

"About what?" Sara asked as she finished filling the bottles for herself and Sage. Juliette was beside them, already watching her bottle turn from cloudy to clear—a sign that it would soon be safe to drink.

"About what comes next," Jonah said.

"I thought that was pretty straightforward," Josh said, chuckling. "We keep walking until we get home and then we sleep for a week." He stretched his arms as if he were yawning.

Jonah turned his head toward the ground and then raised it. "That's my plan too, but is it everyone's?"

Josh's expression fell as he realized what Jonah meant. I wondered if Jonah had read my mind. Josh glanced at Blaise, but her face was hard. She didn't look at him. She looked only at her parents, with her eyes full of hate.

Richard sat up straight. Felicia slumped back.

Everyone knew what this was about. Everyone knew this was a conversation we had to have and everyone had been putting it off for as long as we could. But it was time to make the decision. We couldn't lead them closer, and we would not hurt them or take away their weapons. It was simply time for them to leave, to go their own way.

"Say what you want to say," Richard demanded in frustration.

Jonah locked eyes with Richard. "You've come far enough," he said without hesitation.

"Far enough?" Felicia questioned.

Blaise was silent, her expression unreadable. Josh was upset, but at who, I couldn't tell.

"They don't want us," Richard said coldly to his wife.

Blaise glared at her parents. "Why would they? They don't know you and neither do I," she said.

Her mom leaned toward her. "Blaise, you know us better than anyone. We raised you. We love you," Felicia said, her voice filling with tears.

Blaise squeezed her fists tight, turning her knuckles white. She shouted, "My parents never would have killed that beautiful girl and her parents."

Felicia opened her mouth to speak.

Blaise raised a hand to stop her. She seethed, her tone low and threatening: "You ... murdered ... them."

"It wasn't murder," Felicia said.

Blaise lifted her eyes to her mother's. "Were you not there, Mother? Did you not see yourself fire the gun and see the bullet rip through Annalise? Did you not see her fall? I did!" she shouted. "Every time I close my eyes I see them. Every time I close my eyes I am reminded of the monsters that you are."

"We ... we were doing our job," Felicia said, her head bent toward the ground.

My stomach twisted at her words—the blatant disrespect for life, as if someone telling you to kill somehow made it okay.

"Your job?" Josh said, his face contorted in disgust.

"You have no right to judge us," Richard said. "You have no idea what it was like."

"We do not get to judge your soul and I am grateful for that," Jonah said. "But we have every right to judge your actions. We live in the same world as you. Certain actions demand punishment, and murder is one of those."

"Either we killed or we were killed," Richard said in angry defiance.

"Then—you—die!" Blaise said.

"That's what you want? For your mother and me to be dead?" Richard shouted.

"*My* mother and *my* father are dead, you killed them! You both killed them!" she shouted, and stood, running from us. Josh ran after her.

Richard shook his head in condescension.

I could bite my tongue no longer. "You have no right," I said. "No right to expect her or any of us to welcome you to our home. What you did was disgusting, and to justify murdering a family by saying it was your job is insanity."

"Bria, you're a child," Richard said. "You're all children who have no idea how the world works."

I shook with anger. Jonah sprang to his feet, towering over Richard. Richard stood to match his stance. Jonah's shoulders spanned twice the width of Richard's.

"It is time for you to leave," Jonah said, his voice angry, yet calmer than mine would have been.

Richard glared at him, threw his pack on his back, and held out a hand for his wife to join him. She took his hand and stood, but did not pick up her pack. Instead, she reached for Astrea and petted her silky ears.

"Come on, let's go," Richard said to Felicia.

Her eyes focused on Blaise and Josh in the distance. Josh was holding her. She was crying.

They're right," Felicia said softly. "We killed not in self-defense, but in hatred."

"I didn't hate those people," Richard said.

"Didn't you?" His wife stared into his eyes. "Didn't you think all the slaves were worth less than even a dog? Did it matter to you what happened to them? It didn't matter to me. I killed them, not because someone told me to—though they did—but because there was no reason not to," she said.

Her voice sounded strange, as if she were in shock as she spoke.

He said, "I … what difference does this make? My actions, your actions, they're in the past. We need to focus on the present and the future, not the past."

"The best predictor of future behavior is past behavior," Sage said, her arms crossed as she came to stand beside Jonah and me. Sara and Juliette moved in behind us, and Astrea trotted to Juliette.

"Their deaths saved others from being killed," Richard said flatly.

"That seems unlikely," Sara said, her arms folded, her hard stance matching her sister's.

"By killing them, it kept others in line," Richard said in a matter-of-fact tone. "You saw how smoothly it went when they called for that boy. No one caused any problems. He did as he was told. Lives were saved. They learned from the girl and her family."

"His name was Ryan," Juliette said softly.

"And her name was Annalise," Blaise said as she and Josh returned. "And there was no difference between her and me or her parents and you."

Richard's face contorted. "They were slaves," he said in disgust at his daughter comparing herself to one of them.

"They were people," Jonah said. "With the same worth as you or Blaise, and you killed them."

"I'm sorry," Blaise said through tears. "I'm sorry, but you need to leave."

"Blaise, honey, we love you," Felicia said, placing her hands on her daughter's shoulders.

Blaise sniffed and stepped back, away from her mother's reach. "I know you do, and I have never doubted that, not once in my whole life. But I don't love you, not this you. I'm sorry the world turned you into monsters, but I can't let you be around people I love. Maybe someday we will find one another again, and maybe on that day things will be different, but today you have to leave."

Josh's hand was on her shoulder. Sara looped her hand into hers. We were united in this decision, an inevitable decision none of us had wanted to make.

Four
EAST

"How much longer are we going to wait?" Seth asked.

Had I ever heard him speak in a non-whining tone? I couldn't remember.

"Are you volunteering to break them out?" Jael asked, splotches of sunlight hitting her face, making her expression difficult to interpret.

"Yes, I would rather risk being shot than eat another meal of insects," Seth moaned.

"You read the note," Haz said. "The guy said, wait two days."

"And it's been two days."

"He said he'd signal," Ash said from his place on the ground beside Seth.

Each of us was hidden behind branches that we had collected and put in place slowly, during the first night after we'd signaled the pacing guy. He, unlike us, did have paper and when he came back out the next day he absently tossed it toward us. Once it was dark, Haz retrieved it. It said only: "Wait for my signal in two days."

So here we sat ... waiting. I didn't like it any better than Seth did, but there was no reason to whine about it. It wasn't like we could control how fast the sun set.

"Relax," Ash said. "He said two days. It hasn't been two days."

"We're halfway through the second day," Seth said in frustration.

"Right," I said, "so we have half a day to go."

Seth glared at me. I preferred that to the ogling he typically did.

Ash said, "He'll signal soon, or we'll figure out a different plan."

The guard that sat on the stone wall near the back of the house pulled the walkie-talkie from his belt. He listened, and then put it back and stood, stretching.

"Delivery is here," he called.

I crouched onto my knees, leaning forward. This was different. He and three other guards turned and climbed the embankment toward the front of the house and continued onto the road in front of it. The pacing man continued to pace and neared the only remaining guard. His hands were in his pockets, his head turned toward the ground. The pacing man was behind the guard. He barely veered from his path as he pulled a rag from his pocket and stuffed it in the guard's mouth from behind. The older, senator prisoner was there before the guard could react. He pulled the gun from the guard's belt and held it against the guard's chest. The woman prisoner came forward, string in her hands. She tied his hands as they pushed him toward a pole with a metal loop attached to it. It was meant to be used to tie up horse reins. They tied the man to it. From behind, he would appear to be guarding the prisoners as he was supposed to be doing. The rag stuffed in his mouth kept him from calling out.

We were on our feet, Haz and I moving forward, toward the open field. We stopped as the three prisoners entered the forest.

"We don't have much time," the pacing man said, hurrying forward, and didn't bother to ask who we were or why we were helping him escape.

"The other guards will be back soon," the woman said.

She was as old as my mom, or older. The older senator had a limp. It reminded me of Bria's dad. I wondered if the senator had been shot, also.

Jael and Ash led the way. Haz and I stayed to the back. The pacing man could keep up with at least Seth. The others could not. Their pace was dangerously slow. As we reached the first fence, shots rang out. I turned. I couldn't see the guards yet, but they were there. Haz ran ahead and lifted the fence; it was the same loose spot we had climbed under five days ago. We all dove under the fence and Haz followed.

We were in the open space between the two fences. I did not like this spot. The tall grass did nothing to hide us or protect us from bullets. The guards neared the first fence, firing wildly as they ran. I turned and fired.

Haz lifted the second fence.

The first two prisoners and Jael were through.

"Go," Haz shouted at me.

"No," I shouted back. I didn't want to leave him with the oldest and slowest prisoner and Seth.

"Now!" he ordered.

Shots fired. I looked at Haz and then dove under the fence. I stood and shoved the two prisoners forward. "Move," I commanded.

More shots. I turned. The old senator was crawling under the fence. Too slow, he was going too slow. Haz stood, holding the fence with one hand, shooting his pistol with the other.

Two guards were down. Only one was making his way under the first fence, but others were coming up to it quickly. Seth crawled under. I ran back and fired. The guard at the fence fell, the others weren't there yet. Haz went under, the loose metal falling back into place. Haz's back scraped against it. Seth was pulling the prisoner forward. Haz was almost through. Shots began again and in the background another sound, a hum, like the sound of electricity surging through a machine. I stood, trying to understand the sound.

Haz's body began to shake.

"They energized the fence," Jael yelled from behind me.

Haz's body continued to convulse.

"No!" I screamed, and ran toward him.

Someone ran beside me. It was the "pacing" prisoner and he was pulling off his shirt. I bent to pull Haz forward. Electricity surged through my body and I fell back, slamming into Ash. The prisoner tied his shirt around Haz's hand and pulled him forward. Ash threw me to my feet and went to the man, helping him drag Haz from the fence. Haz was clear. The guards ran to the fence. Bullets whizzed around us.

The prisoner knelt by Haz. "He's alive, but barely," he shouted. "Help me."

He and Ash lifted Haz. I returned fire and Jael did the same. I hit a guard, she hit another. Four more remained.

Jael shoved her gun between her waist and her pants. She lifted Haz's legs. I continued firing, my back to the others, keeping the guards from getting a clear shot. Trees covered us overhead as one of the guards charged the fence. He hadn't seen what it did to Haz and he was oblivious to the humming that surrounded us. He was thrown backward, falling to the ground.

We were safe for the moment. I turned and grasped one of Haz's legs from Jael's grip. We needed to run and we did.

"They have vehicles," the prisoner carrying Haz said. "We have to hurry."

It would take us a full day to make it back to town, longer if we were limited by the slow pace of the limping prisoner and longer still if we were carrying Haz. But we weren't going back to town, not yet. The ground was dropping beneath us; a steep incline on the way up was an even steeper decline on the way down. Ash tripped. The others, including Haz, fell, tumbling down the hill. I allowed myself to slide so I could stay with them.

In the distance, several dogs barked. My body shivered and turned rigid. I loved animals, but I hated dogs. They terrified me at a level nothing else did. I understood where the fear came from. I also understood I needed to work to get over that fear. But something told me these dogs were the kind it was all right to be scared of.

Their barking sounded louder. They would have no trouble tracking us; our scent was everywhere. The others had stopped rolling down the hill. It was good they fell. It got us down the hill faster than we would have done otherwise. I went to them. Haz lay motionless. He had rolled limply to a stop. It was a blessing, I guessed, that he was already unconscious when he fell; his body would not be fighting to stop the fall and so would not be too bruised. Though if he had been conscious, he never would have fallen down the hill in the first place.

I turned him over, placing my fingers under his nose. I felt the warm breath. I rubbed his short beard, hoping it might wake him, but it didn't. The dogs barked, and terror ran through me. I wished he would wake up. We had prisoners to rescue and ourselves to keep alive, and without him to help, that was all far less likely. I had come to count on him, on his stability. I appreciated him so much for that. I wondered if it was his police training that kept him calm when our lives were in danger or if he had always been that way.

Jael, Ash, and Seth were standing, brushing dirt from their clothes.

"They have dogs," Jael said. "We need to cover our scent."

"How're we supposed to do that?" Seth snapped.

"I hear water," Jael said.

I listened. I heard it too. The quiet rushing of a mountain stream. Ash sprinted away and then returned.

"Come on, I have an idea," he said.

I helped carry Haz along with Seth, Jael, and Ash. Even with the extra weight, we were still faster than the old man and woman.

I was wrong. It was not a stream; it was a tranquil waterfall making its way down the same hill we had come down.

"Cover yourselves with mud from the bottom of the stream, not the bank," Ash said, as the frigid water encased my shoes.

The water seeped into my shoes and permeated my socks. As a child, I had loved that feeling. But then, we didn't have to walk everywhere we went. Now the feel of wet feet meant blisters would soon cover them.

We laid Haz in the stream. I kept his head above water as Jael scooped mud, covering his body.

"You, come're," Seth called to the pacing prisoner.

Both of them were dry, neither covered in mud.

With apprehension, the prisoner replied, "Why?"

"Don't ask questions. Run over there and run back, try to stay on your original path."

The man did as he was told. Seth ran in another direction. I understood then that they were creating trails for the dogs to follow. It was a surprisingly good idea.

"There's no more time for that," Jael said. "We have to find cover."

Seth and the man jumped into the stream and covered themselves in as much mud as they could, while Ash ran to the base of the falls.

"Here," Ash said.

It wasn't a cave, but it wasn't open space, either. It was a little rock alcove off the front of the falls. It was all we had and I prayed it would be enough. We hauled Haz into the space, laying him as far against the rocks as we could.

"Now what?" the woman prisoner asked.

"We wait," Jael said. Dogs barked in the distance. "It won't be a long wait."

Her voice was steady, but I heard the fear. I could always hear the fear.

Five
BRIA

The mountains were long gone. Low hills provided our sanctuary. There had been no helicopters or signs of the new government for at least a week. We saw indications of humans, but they were few and infrequent. Without humans to compete with or control them, the animal predators were thriving. From the scat they left and the shadows we glimpsed, there were many and they were large, but they stayed in the shadows.

The last few days—since we forced Richard and Felicia to leave—had been difficult for Blaise. She was mourning the loss of her parents. Though they weren't dead, in some ways she thought it might be better if they were. Sara and I told her she was wrong about this, but she reminded us that our moms had done all they could to save lives, not destroy them. She was right; Sara and I had no idea how she felt. I could compare what her parents had done to what my father did all those years, but even his betrayal didn't dig that deep. Richard and Felicia truly believed there was nothing wrong with their actions. That hurt the most—or, at least, was what disgusted me the most.

"They're still following us," Jonah said softly as he walked beside me.

"What are we going to do?" I asked, casually turning my head to try to glimpse them.

"Does Blaise know?" he asked.

I turned back. I couldn't see them. "I haven't told her and she hasn't realized. None of them have."

Jonah somehow saw things that the rest of us didn't. He said it was the result of growing up outside and noticing when things were out of place. I wondered if it had something to do with all the praying he did. Maybe God gave him some sort of superpowered vision to say thanks for all the prayers. I'd told Sara about this theory once when Jonah noticed a game trail that the rest of us missed. I expected her to dismiss it for the joke that it was, but she hadn't. She merely said that was possible, not as a thank-you gift from God, but as a result of being more tuned in to him. From that point on, I started paying more attention and I realized that Jonah was almost always the one who located the game we would later eat or the berries we would gratefully consume. This time he had not noticed food, but enemies.

When Richard and Felicia left, they did not go far. It had been difficult for Blaise to see their campfire in the distance. The next day we hoped they had moved on, but as the day went on Jonah told me they were still back there. The next day had been no different and, today, on the third day, they still remained. They could not be allowed to continue following us. We could not allow them to go to our home.

We didn't want to hurt them, but we could not allow them to hurt our families. If they were near them, we would be taking that risk.

"We need to tell her," Jonah said as we neared the others.

"Tell who what?" Sage asked.

I bit my lip and locked eyes with Blaise. "Your parents are following us."

"They're what?" she said, with the edge of anger that now defined her voice.

Jonah nodded. "They're about a mile behind us."

"I can't see them," Josh said, craning his neck.

"From here you can't," Jonah acknowledged, "but when I stay back, I catch a glimpse of them every once in a while."

"That's it!" Blaise screamed. She stormed past Jonah, retracing our steps, not trying to be quiet about it.

The rest of us followed, each telling her to calm down and that we should figure out a plan. But she didn't listen.

In only a few minutes we saw them coming around the side of a hill. Their faces registered shock when they saw us.

"Why are you following us?" Blaise yelled, her body shaking with anger.

I was glad we were so far in the middle of nowhere. She was being too loud. She would have given away our position if there was anyone within miles to give it away to.

Richard stepped forward, his head lowered. "To tell you you're right."

None of us spoke. Blaise's breathing was heavy and fast.

Felicia took Richard's hand in hers. "We don't understand," she said, "why we did what we did."

"What you did was murder," Blaise said, her voice quieter but no less rage-filled.

Felicia flinched at the word.

"Yes," Richard said. "It was."

Blaise's posture softened slightly.

"We cannot offer you an explanation," Richard said, "we don't have one. We spent the last three days trying to understand why we killed them, why we saw nothing wrong with our actions, and we have no better understanding than we did two days ago."

"Blaise," her mother said, "we're monsters, and we accept if you never want to see us again. But we had to at least tell you that you're right to leave us behind."

Felicia's tears were building. "We also had to tell you we love you and we have never, from the first second we held you in our arms, ever stopped loving you and … we are so sorry." Her tears fell as Richard put an arm around her shoulders.

Jonah stepped forward. "Give me your guns," he demanded, his hand outstretched.

Everyone stared at him. Richard took the gun from his waistband and handed it to him. Felicia did the same. Jonah slipped them into his pack.

"We can't spend the rest of the day here as you examine your consciences. Examine while we walk," he said, turning and beginning to move forward.

Richard stared in confusion. "You're allowing us to go with you?"

Josh took Blaise's hand. The two turned, following Jonah's lead. "For now," Josh said.

Six
EAST

The prisoners sat, covered in mud, huddled like children, behind us. They trusted us to keep them alive. I couldn't do that—trust total strangers to keep me alive. It was good, I guess, that they could still trust.

The dogs were close ... their masters with them, the human footsteps heavy and sloppy. It was clear they didn't hunt their food. They never would've eaten.

My head pressed against the stone, the handle of my pistol in the palm of my right hand. It was pointed toward the sky. I was close to the opening, but not the closest. That was Jael and Ash. No matter the risk, they took it. They were courageous to a degree I doubted I would ever be.

If Haz were awake, he would've forced himself in front of me and I would've let him. Not because I was scared, but because he was better trained than me. Jael and Ash were too. The three of them were true soldiers. I watched them whenever I could, to learn the subtleties of what they did: how they held their weapons and their bodies. I had improved a few of my techniques, but they were still better. Back at the town, Jael and I had often fought for fun, never to hurt one another. She tried to teach me, but so much of what she did was second nature to her that she had forgotten learning it and so she struggled to teach me.

She was a good friend, and I was grateful to have her. Not only because she was a better fighter, but when Sara left, I lost my best friend. Jael and Haz had become the closest thing to family I had. Though, there were things I could talk to Jael about that I couldn't talk to Haz about. Most specifically, I could talk to Jael about Haz and while I tried not to make him the focus of our conversations, he often was.

Jael said he was into me. I told her she was wrong—but she was right. It was obvious. I wished he wasn't so handsome or that I wasn't so focused on appearances. If either of those things changed, it would be easier for me to ignore him and his interest in me. As it was, I was too focused on him.

I glanced at Haz's motionless body and then turned away.

The dogs were at the stream. My body began to sweat. *They're not Wrath. Wrath is dead,* I thought over and over again while trying to calm myself. I hated that dogs terrified me. It was a weakness and a significant one. When we got back to town, I'd force myself to pet HoneyBee and Jasper. I wouldn't allow myself to hide from them any longer. My body shuddered as I heard the dogs splash into the water.

I closed my eyes and prayed again for protection. I prayed that they would not find us. I prayed that the dogs followed the false trails of Seth and the prisoner. *Please, God, don't let them find us, but if they do, let us kill them first.* I never would have thought it okay to pray to kill someone, if my grandfather had not been murdered by a sociopath. Now when I prayed for protection for myself and those I cared about, I understood that meant someone else might be harmed or even killed.

The dogs whined in frustration. The trail was lost, as we had hoped. One dog bayed. A guard ran loudly behind him. The dog was pulling him away, down the hill. Another dog followed, and then another. Three dogs and guards were gone. How many guards were there?

I hurriedly wiped the sweat from my right palm onto a rock. It was damp, but not covered in mud like everything else. The gun was back in my hand. *How long do we wait?* I wanted to ask the question, but didn't dare speak. My breath caught as I heard the splash of a man's foot in the water. Followed by another splash ... and another. One of them was coming toward us. My gaze darted to Jael. Ash handed her his gun. They exchanged a glance, and I prayed for their safety, for all of our safety.

The water near our sandy embankment moved ... the ripples splashing closer toward us than those from the waterfall.

A crack between some rocks allowed us to see a man's face. Ash stepped forward. His hands lifted and in a smooth

39

motion he brought the man to the soggy sand, twisting his neck in the process. I aimed my gun at his chest. Ash released the man to the sand and stood over him.

"He's dead," Jael whispered as she pushed my gun out of the way.

Seth pulled the man's body into the alcove. A gold cross hung loosely from the chain on his broken neck. I closed my eyes. I prayed for his soul and for ours. We had no choice, but every death brought me tremendous pain. As it should, the loss of human life was never to be celebrated. I wanted so badly to go to confession, to feel the weight of my actions lifted. In some ways I thought I was made to be a warrior, to fight and defend, but then I was forced to see death and I was sure I was not made for this kind of life. I wondered if anyone was.

I turned my eyes from the dead man and the gold cross hanging from his neck. For some reason, that made the killing worse, though I wasn't sure why. All life was equally sacred, regardless of the religion they followed or the god they believed in.

In the back of the alcove, Haz was sitting up. *Thank you,* I prayed. The woman prisoner tried to calm him, whispering that he was safe for the moment. He was confused and terrified. He found my eyes. I lifted a finger to my lips, begging him to be quiet. His expression shifted. He was no longer terrified. I was with him and that made things better for him. His presence did the same for me.

Haz's gaze fell on the dead man at our feet. Haz was sorry for his death; I could see it in his eyes.

"Come on," Ash said, and Jael signaled for us to follow them.

Seth went after them, slipping behind the narrow falls. The prisoners followed.

I knelt, unable to stop myself. I closed the dead man's eyes and traced a small cross on his forehead.

"May God have mercy on his soul," Haz whispered as he pulled me up.

"I'm glad you're alive," I said.

"Me too," he said as we left the rocks.

"Why am I covered in mud?"

"You smelled bad," I whispered, teasing.

His eyes ran down my mud-splattered body. "Apparently, you did too."

"Apparently," I said, raising my hand toward his beard. I stopped. The dried mud appeared gray against his dark skin.

"What?" he asked in confusion.

What was I doing? I had no idea. "Nothing. Just glad you aren't dead," I said.

The cold water refocused my mind. It ran through my shoes, up to my shins. Haz stayed beside me as the others led the way.

We ran in silence, away from the stream, and continued to move away from Camp David—but not in the direction we had been going. We were backtracking. It made sense. They wouldn't expect us to go back the way we'd come.

Water squeezed itself from my shoes with each step, making too much noise. There were eight of us, making too much noise. We wouldn't be difficult to find, out in the open like this. We needed to reach our shelters.

We decided before we went to Camp David that we wouldn't go directly back to town. It would leave us out in the open and vulnerable for far too long, and we ran the risk of being followed and not even realizing it. As much as I didn't want to be captured or killed, I didn't want to endanger Momma Pryce and the others. If the guards wanted, they could keep their distance and watch as we led them straight back to the rest of the town.

Thankfully, this area had many natural and manmade hiding options. We had left enough provisions for a week in three different locations. We weren't sure how many prisoners we would have with us and it's easier to hide a small number of people rather than a big group.

We'd split up soon and not be back together until we got to the town. It wouldn't take long to get there. Two days at the most, but we'd spend at least a day in hiding.

I caught myself as my knees hit the ground. I'd been knocked from behind. I turned, ready to fight. Haz was beside me.

"Sorry," he said as he picked himself up from the ground.

"What happened?" I asked. When I got up, layers of mud crumbled off my pants and shirt.

"I'm not sure," he said, rubbing his temples. "I'm tired, I guess."

"You were electrocuted," the woman prisoner said. "You need to rest."

"She's right," Ash said. "You take the high cave. It's the closest by miles."

Haz propped himself up against a tree. "No, I'm okay. I can keep going."

Even as he said it his knees buckled, and he had to grab onto the tree to keep from falling into the dirt.

"I'll stay with him. The rest of you go," I said.

Jael glanced from me to the prisoners. "You, what's your name?" she asked the man who had been pacing.

"John," he answered.

"Can you shoot?" she asked.

"I learned as a kid."

"That'll have to do. The others would be no help to you," Jael said to me. "John, go with East and Haz," Jael said. She glanced at Haz's weapon and made a face, as if to say something, but thought better of it.

"Go where?" John asked.

"We're splitting up," Ash said. "We'll meet back at our home. He needs to rest and she's going to need help with him."

"I'll be fine," I said, offended that they thought I couldn't take care of Haz.

"We don't have time for your grandiosity," Seth said as he started to walk away. "John, go with them."

"He's so irritating," I whispered to Jael as she gave me a hug.

"Yeah, but he's right about this one. You're going to need all the help you can get," she said, appraising Haz, who was leaning heavily against the tree. "Be careful, okay?"

I nodded as she released me.

"I'll stay with them," the woman prisoner said from her place beside John.

"Nope," Jael said, "you're coming with me and my brother. You," she said, pointing at the older man, "you can go with Seth."

I felt bad for that man.

"No," the woman said, "I'm staying with John."

Jael stood in front of the woman. "Nope, you're with me."

The woman was nervous, scared, even.

"Smaller numbers increase our chances of survival," Jael said in a voice that was meant to be kind but sounded harsh if you didn't know her. "You'll be safe with us—unless the dogs come back before we get out of here."

The woman stared at Jael and then back at John.

"It's okay, Pam, I'll meet you back at their camp," he said, and gave her a hug.

She was terrified to be separated from him. The feeling was not mutual. She meant little to him—not that he didn't care what happened to her. He did, but her life didn't affect his. He was fine separating from her. But she was not okay with this. He was younger than her and stronger than her. His eyes burned with life in a way that many eyes did not. It made him attractive, but that wasn't why she wanted to stay with him. She didn't think of him in that way.

She appeared as if she was about to cry, but didn't. I wondered how long they had known each other: were they involved in some way before they were prisoners, or were her reasons for needing him because they had been together in their confinement?

The older man reached out a hand to John. "Good luck," he said.

John grasped his hand and the two locked eyes. "You too," John said to the man as they released.

They were not friends. Though again, it was the other prisoner who cared more for John. He was at least sincere in his wishing of good luck. John—if my gut was right—wished him anything but luck.

"Let's go," Jael ordered as she began down the hill.

The others followed. For an instant, Jonah and my friends replaced their fading images, and tears threatened. I wished my mind wouldn't do that—replace one thing for another. It didn't happen as much as it used to, but when it did, it brought up so many emotions, none of which I wanted. I shook my head and refocused. The others continued down the hill.

"Can you keep going?" I asked Haz.

He appeared weak, but he nodded.

"Here. Lean on me if you need to," John said, moving close to Haz.

"I'm okay," Haz said, stepping away from the tree.

I led us forward. After a few feet I heard John helping Haz. I turned. Haz's arm was around John's neck. He didn't like accepting help from anyone. We were alike in that way. Their pace was steady but slow. I carried my pistol and Haz carried his, though I doubted he could've hit anything in his current state.

If shooting started, I would tell John to take Haz's weapon. Though something about John told me he was smart enough to figure that out without being told. Maybe it was intelligence or maybe it was a desire to live. Either way, I was glad he was with us. Of the three, he seemed the most capable of actually contributing in some way. I was grateful to Jael for sending him with me.

I tried not to glance up the hill where the guards would be coming from. Thank God it was summer and not fall or winter, when we could've been seen from miles in any direction. With the full greenery of bushes and leaves, it would be difficult for anyone to see us unless they were near. But it would also be difficult for us to see them unless they were already close enough for one of their bullets to hit us.

My stomach growled. I was starving, literally. We had not anticipated waiting five full days to free John and the others. The packs we carried were light, with only three days' worth of minimal provisions. We'd done what we could to make them last. We supplemented with insects, but it had been two days since I ate anything more than a few earthworms. The lack of food was overpowering the adrenaline, causing my senses to dull.

I wondered how Haz was still going. He hadn't eaten any more than me and he had been electrocuted.

"There it is," I said as the vegetation gave way to rocks at our feet and rocks beside us, a vertical wall of probably thirty or forty feet. Halfway up, going back into the hill, was an opening. I had been the one who scouted it. Haz and I were both good climbers, but I was better—at least when I wasn't starving.

"Where?" John said, glancing around.

I pointed up. He said nothing. I wondered if he could climb. By his lack of response, I doubted it.

"We left a rope," I said.

Haz lowered himself onto a rock. He would be no help; he was too weak to protect me. Too weak to keep his gun from John and too weak to hit anything or anyone if he needed to defend me as I climbed.

I went to John. "Tell me a reason I should trust you," I said, staring into his eyes.

He didn't shift his gaze or appear confused. He understood why I asked.

"I love my wife with every ounce of my being. Our kids are our world. Every breath I take without them hurts more than I ever thought I could hurt, and my body and soul cry out for death so the pain will stop. But I refuse to die"—his voice rose with determination—"I have to believe they are still alive, and I will fight for them and for the life that we had. A life that was defined by love, not hate. I will fight that hate with the love of my wife, the love of my son, and the love of my daughter, and I will not let this world change me. I will be with them someday and it will be as the father and as the husband they loved, not as someone who sold his soul to this world."

I longed to be home. I longed to hug my parents and my sister. I took the gun from my waistband.

"Don't let them shoot me or him," I said, handing it to him.

He nodded as the gun slipped from my fingers.

The rocks were dry, the afternoon sun beating against them. It felt good to climb; it's where I felt peace. Suspended above the earth, with only my toes and fingertips tying me to it. I lifted myself onto the narrow ledge and scooted inside. The thin material of my shirt offered little comfort from the small rocks sliding under my stomach and arms. Once inside the opening, I was able to crawl. I found the packs where I had left them.

As I dug for the rope, I found dried meat and hungrily shoved a piece into my mouth. I took time chewing it, allowing the taste to fill my mouth as I found the rope. I tied one end around my waist and threw the other end down. I lay on my stomach so I could see John and Haz beneath me. Haz was slumped on the flat rock. Conscious, but just barely. John was scanning the trees around them, making sure no one was coming.

"Send the gun up first," I said.

John took the rope and tied it through the handle of the gun. I was soon untying it and dropping the rope back to John.

"Tie it around your waist," I said.

"No, he should go first," John said, handing the rope to Haz.

Haz was sitting on the rock, his head leaning against a tree trunk. He needed rest and food. He held his gun, though he'd not be able to hit anything.

I shook my head. "I'll need you to help me pull him up if he falls."

Haz weighed a lot more than me and with the force of gravity, I doubted I could stop him from falling and taking me with him. John, on the other hand, was closer to my size. I could pull him up if I had to, and he could help.

Haz must have agreed. He handed the rope back to John, who looped it around his waist twice.

"Ready?" he asked.

"Yes," I said, and turned around, scooting back and bracing my feet against the walls of the cave. I inched backward, keeping the slack as tight as possible.

The rope wasn't needed. He made it up. Drenched in sweat, red-faced, and out of breath, he crawled onto the ledge. He struggled to untie the rope around his waist. Finally, it was free.

I scooted to the mouth of the cave. My head hung over the edge as I stared down at Haz. He took the rope and tied it around his waist, and then dropped his pistol into his bag before slipping the bag onto his back. He lifted his head toward me and took a tired breath.

I called down to him, "It'll be okay. Take your time."

"Yeah, 'cause we both know how patient you are," he said, his words slow and deliberate.

I appreciated his sarcasm; it told me he was not as beaten as he seemed.

I turned around, inching backward, careful to brace myself against the cave walls. John was trying to guide him while leaning over the edge, my pistol at his side. I was nearing the halfway mark of the cave. It couldn't be much longer. A shot rang out and the line became tight. I slid forward, the loose gravel cutting against my back as my shirt lifted, the ground pushing it up. Another shot. My feet found the side of the cave. I pushed, my quads burning as I lifted Haz upward. *Dear God, let the rope hold. Dear God, let Haz be okay.*

John had fired the second shot. The echo of the bullet leaving the barrel was deafening in the narrow cave. Reaching his hand down, John placed the gun beside him and helped lift Haz. Haz scrambled to the top and slid into the cave. John followed behind him.

I loosened the rope from my waist and crawled to Haz. My back and obliques felt bruised from the pull of the rope. My legs burned, but Haz was here and he was conscious and I saw no massive blood loss. If he'd been shot, it wasn't a bad wound.

"Are you okay?" I asked.

Haz nodded.

"He was shot," John said.

Haz straightened his leg. "A flesh wound," he said.

In the dim light I could see the torn cloth, already soaked red, on his upper thigh. I turned to the pack and pulled out a dingy plastic bottle full of clear liquid.

"We have to clean it."

Haz didn't move. His fingers tightened into fists. I took the cap from the bottle. The smell of rubbing alcohol made my empty stomach hurt. I avoided his eyes as I poured some of the alcohol onto the wound. His body became rigid and he sucked in air. I closed the bottle. Haz bounced his leg in an attempt to dry the alcohol. I felt bad he was in pain, but he would feel worse if it became infected. I returned the bottle to the pack and crawled to the opening of the cave—careful to stay in the shadows.

I saw no one. In the distance, the dogs barked. If they were able to smell our scent beneath the mud, they would be able to track us to the rocks at the base of this cliff. If this happened, we would likely die. As good a hiding place as this was, it did not have an easy escape route. We would address that when we needed to. I would not worry about things I had no control over.

I crawled back to Haz.

"Who shot you?" I asked.

He shrugged, his hands holding his leg tight. I wondered if the wound still stung from the alcohol or if he was trying to slow the minor blood loss.

"One of the guards," John said. "I hit him in the chest. I don't think he'll live long."

"Let's hope he dies before he can tell anyone else where we are," Haz said, resting his head against the damp stone wall. His hands loosened a little. I took that as a sign that the pain must be subsiding.

John said, "It's difficult for me to hope for someone's death, even someone like that."

He reminded me of Eli and Sara, not only in his words but in his presence. This similarity made me like him.

"Here, take some," I said, offering strips of meat to Haz and John. I pulled out a liter bottle of water. I took a drink. There were five more, three in each pack. I gave one to each of them and chewed some meat.

"What do we do now?" John asked as he tore a piece of the meat, chewing hungrily.

"We wait," I said.

"How long?" he asked.

"As long as it takes for us to be able to leave here safely," I answered.

"How long do you think that will be?" John asked, swallowing what he chewed and taking another bite.

"Hopefully, no longer than a few days," I said. "Much longer than that and we'll run out of food."

Haz's eyes were heavy with sleep. He had taken only one bite of the meat and one gulp of water. I hit his foot with mine. "Take another bite of food and crawl over there. Where you'll be out of sight."

He tore another piece of jerky with his teeth and methodically chewed as he crawled behind a jagged wall of rocks. The cave was larger than it appeared from the outside.

"Will we be safe here?" John asked, his face turned toward the opening of the cave.

"As long as the guard you shot doesn't tell the others where we are," I answered.

"So if he's dead, we have a chance to live, but if he lives, we die," John said, turning to me.

"Yes," I answered. "That seems to be how things work in this world," I said, positioning myself so I could see the mouth of the cave while keeping most of my body hidden.

"And you don't like it?" he asked, with what sounded like cautious hope in his voice.

"No, I don't like it," I said as I chewed the last bit of the meat I held.

Seven
BRIA

"Do you see that?" Sara said, a raised hand pointing above the trees.

From a sea of green leaves, two gray spires rose toward the heavens. On top of each, metal glistened in the sunlight.

"What is it?" Josh asked.

"It looks old, whatever it is," I said, noticing the strange way one of the spires was taller than the other. They were so close to one another they must be part of the same building.

"I think it's a church," Jonah said, a hint of something in his voice that I didn't recognize. Excitement was part of it, but there was more.

"A church? We're nowhere near anywhere," Sage said.

"Yeah, I know," Jonah said.

This time I understood the other emotion; it was hope.

"Who would build a church out here?" Felicia asked.

"Monks," Jonah said as he moved swiftly forward, forcing the rest of us to try to keep pace.

Sunlight shone brightly a few yards in front of us. Jonah stopped, staring at the stone building surrounded by a field of tall grasses. Wildflowers sprinkled here and there reminded me of Quinn and JP when they had placed delicate flowers in

Blaise's braid on her wedding day. Astrea stood between Jonah and me, waiting for Jonah to lead her.

Each of us stared at the church. There was no sign of life. The grass was tall and there were no paths through it. If humans had walked near here within the last week or so, we would see the grasses trampled.

"That looks like a game trail," Josh said, pointing to the far side of the field. There the meadow was marked with a thin line of broken grasses.

"I agree," Jonah said, though I wondered if he had even seen it, he was so focused on the church.

He was ready to run. I reached for his hand to hold him back, to remind him that we must be cautious.

"There's an old cemetery," Sage said, gesturing to the back edge of the building.

A short metal fence enclosed gray stones standing in erratic rows. Gravestones.

Jonah stepped forward.

I pulled him back into the trees. "You can't," I said, the stone walls of the building making me nervous. I couldn't see beyond them. "Anyone could be in there. They could be watching us."

"Do you not feel it?" he asked, half looking at me, half looking through me, toward the church.

Astrea whined. Did she think we should go or did she think we should stay? I couldn't tell.

"Feel what?" I asked, my nervousness growing.

Astrea whined again. Juliette came to her and placed a hand on her back. Astrea calmed.

Jonah turned to me. "I can't describe it. It's like a magnet pulling me in."

"That makes no sense," I whispered.

He bent and kissed me. "I realize that," he said, pulling away from me.

My hand grasped for his, but it was gone. He was gone. Before I could do or say anything, he was in the open, out of the shelter of the trees. My heart beat so fast it made thought difficult.

I sprinted behind him, the others calling in whispers for us to return.

"Where're you going?" Josh said.

"Come back," Blaise begged.

They were right. We shouldn't be going forward. We should have waited, and watched and made sure no one was there. But Jonah was running at full speed toward the stone building, and I ran behind him. Astrea must have pulled free from Juliette; the dog was in front of me, going toward Jonah. When my feet hit the cracked cement, I slowed and held my gun with both hands. It was the only way to hit anything I might aim at. But Jonah didn't slow. He bounded up the stone steps, his fingers gliding up the metal railing.

57

He stopped at the door. The palm of his hand reached toward the hand-hewn oak. He flattened it against the centuries-old door, leaning his forehead against his hand. It was oddly intimate and I felt as though I had invaded something that was not mine to be a part of. He lifted his head and placed his hand on the handle. The handle didn't match the door. The door was old and solid, with giant iron hinges that reminded me of something on a castle. The handle was a modern addition, tacky and utilitarian, that didn't belong on this majestic building.

"Jonah, please," I begged, my hand on his, trying to pull it from the door. "Please wait. We don't know what or who is in there."

"It's okay. I promise," he said.

"You don't know that," I said, still pulling his hand away from the door.

He lifted my hand to his lips, kissing the back of it. "I do," he said, releasing my hand and opening the door before I could stop him.

I lifted my gun and lowered my body, preparing to fire at whatever might lie inside the unknown darkness. Jonah continued forward. I heard his footsteps as my eyes struggled to adjust to the darkness. I stepped forward into the shadows. Splotches of light filled my vision. I blinked to clear them. Jonah continued forward, pausing at a white basin. He touched his fingers to it and continued forward, Astrea close beside him. I stood and followed, hearing the footsteps of the others echoing on the stone steps behind me.

The wooden benches, or pews, were perfect for people to hide in or under. With each step Jonah took, I feared that would be the row that contained a threat. Astrea remained by his side. If she were not a puppy, if she understood the world better, her presence beside him would bring me comfort. But as it was, it brought no comfort. She understood more about the world than she did a month ago, but not enough to keep him safe. She followed us blindly. If we said it was okay, she believed us; she was too young to realize we could be wrong, that we could lead her astray.

"What's he doing?" Josh whispered behind me.

"Risking his life and ours," Blaise answered in justified irritation.

I was glad they were there. Glad I was not alone in this massive gothic building with Jonah and hidden danger. Sunlight filtered in through the colored glass, filling the tall structure with reds, blues, golds, and all the shades in between.

When I reached Jonah, he was standing in a beam of red, his face appearing pink beneath its tint.

"Jonah, please," I begged, trying to pull him back, to slow him down. My gun was poised, ready to fire, as I scanned up and down the aisles. I prayed we were alone, while aware there were places people could hide and I'd be unaware of them.

"It's okay, Bria. I'm sure it's okay."

There was no way for him to be sure of that. He wanted it to be okay, to be safe. To him, this place represented all that was good. But our hopes didn't matter. Not anymore.

The shadows moved and I swiveled. Jonah stopped as a rat ran across the floor.

"Astrea, heel," Juliette commanded. Astrea obeyed, going obediently to her master. Our friends came behind us, each holding a weapon, ready to fire. Only Jonah had his against his hip.

"Just a rat," I said, more to myself than to anyone else.

"This time," Blaise whispered. "What about over there … or over there … or over there?" She pointed to the three ends of the church.

I realized then, the church was in the shape of a cross.

"I'm telling you it's fine. There's nothing to be scared of," Jonah said, not bothering to quiet his voice.

"Has he lost his mind?" Josh asked.

I wanted to say yes, but instead I continued checking the pews for threats. With each row, my anxiety subsided by increments. Josh and Blaise angled toward the left side of the cross and her parents went to the right. The others remained behind me, in the center aisle.

I ran in front of Jonah, blocking him with my body.

"It's okay, Bria," he said, trying to push me to one side.

"No!" I said. "No, you will not go up on that stage."

"It's called an altar," he said.

"Whatever, you can't go up there until they've finished searching the church," I said, aware that from the altar he could be seen and shot from any place in the building.

"There's no one here," Blaise called, as Jonah was still trying to get around me.

"See, I told you," Jonah said as he dodged my grasp and approached the altar steps. He bowed as if in an old movie, and raced up the stairs. Sara followed him, copying his actions.

"What're they doing?" Sage asked from beside me.

As they went toward the long table at the front of the church, I allowed my focus to shift, my eyes scanning not for threat but for understanding. This place meant more to them than the memories contained in an ancient place of worship. They were searching for something more than memories. It was what Jonah felt was calling to him, propelling him forward. Behind the table, they knelt at the base of a gold-colored box with a key sticking out of it. Like a dollhouse covered in gold.

"I'm not sure," I said to Sage.

We watched Jonah stand and turn the key … open the box … his hand disappeared inside it. Seconds passed until he pulled out his hand. I tried to see what he held. When he

61

relaxed his hand, I realized he held nothing. His head dropped in defeat. Sara placed a hand on his shoulder. He placed his hands on the top of the box, his head sinking into his outstretched arms. Sara's hand remained on his back as he stood, unmoving, for several minutes. Finally, he lifted his head and closed the box. He allowed his hand to slide from it in a deliberate fashion, as if releasing something he didn't want to release or accepting something he didn't want to accept. He turned toward us, his face distraught. Sara was upset, but not as much as Jonah was.

My heart broke for him, though it made no sense. I wondered what he hoped was there, that wasn't.

"Are you okay?" I asked as he made his way down the stairs, toward me.

"I'll be fine," he said as he turned from me.

Sara stopped in front of me as Jonah went to a pew on the right side of the church and sat down. His gaze focused on the life-sized crucifix that hung above us.

Sara saw the concern and confusion in my eyes.

I turned to her. "What was he doing?" I asked.

"He hoped there were some consecrated hosts," she said.

"The Eucharist?" I said. "That's what he was searching for?"

She nodded. "It's been a long time since we've received. It would've been nice to be so close to Jesus," she said with sad longing as she went to a pew behind me.

With an expression of concern, Sage followed her.

Jonah's face remained lifted, staring at his crucified Savior, and I understood something I hadn't understood before.

I went to him. "You believe it, don't you?" I said as I sat beside him.

"What?" he asked, struggling to meet my gaze.

"All of it," I said. "All the stuff Eli talks about and Sara talks about. Everything." I gestured to the holy scenes in the stained-glass windows and sculptures scattered throughout the church.

Our eyes locked and in that instant I saw him differently. Not as the man I loved, but as the man who loved and was loved by a God I didn't know or understand. A God I could somehow see in Jonah.

"Yeah, I believe it all," Jonah said. "Does that make you think I'm crazy?"

I placed my hand on his face. His beard was soft, the whites of his eyes red, making the green of his irises fade and become more vivid at the same time.

He turned away from me as if embarrassed. And I realized he thought I was staring at him because I was concerned for his sanity, when really I was trying desperately to understand what he understood.

"No. It makes me think you're beautiful," I said softly, my voice catching as I felt myself falling so deeply in love I would never be able to pull myself out.

He turned to me, his expression confused.

I kept my hand on his face and leaned my body toward his. "I have never loved you more than I do right now."

"Really?"

"Jonah, I've never met anyone like you, and when I think I understand you, you show me more of yourself and I fall in love all over again."

From across the church came a mesmerizing sound I hadn't heard since before the light. My hand slid from Jonah's face as I turned. Sunlight filtered through the stained-glass that covered the piano with golds and reds. Juliette's small frame was barely visible. I stood without realizing it and began my way to her. Jonah's hand slipped over mine as we went toward her. Neither of us spoke—neither of us able to. She was playing softly so the sound could not be heard outside of the walls, or at least not past the clearing. The others were already there beside her. The piano was the color of honey. Its finish was worn in some places and still shiny in others.

Perhaps it was this place—the beauty of the structure or the colored glass and marble statues—or perhaps it was that music was part of each of us at a level that can't be explained, but the notes she played made every other awareness fall away. She played in a way that embodied grace and skill, natural talent mixing with years of study and dedication. It was like nothing I'd ever heard, even when my father made my nannies take me to the symphony. Nothing I had heard there came close to what I heard now from an old piano—in an even older church—played by a young girl.

We surrounded her, though she had no idea. Her eyes were closed, her fingers moving as if enchanted. Her mind was somewhere else, her awareness far away from this abandoned church in the middle of an abandoned world. My body filled and emptied based on the notes she played. I could think only of the music, of the power it possessed. From somewhere beside me I heard crying. It was Sage and Felicia. I bit my lip to try to contain the emotion, emotion that came from somewhere hidden even from myself. Memories of joy and pain, of love and hate, swirled together with the music that permeated this space.

Jonah's hand rested on my shoulder and I turned, clutching him, wanting more of him. He returned my grasp, as if we both understood that without the other we would slip away, turning into nothing more than sounds controlled by this magical child who controlled each of us.

After a time the notes slowed, turning into a tune I had heard before, though it was years ago. It took me a minute, but I recognized the sound, slow and rhythmic, mournful in a way I didn't remember it, but that it was.

Juliette's expression turned to one of pained sorrow as she captured all the hurt of the world and placed it into this one song. As "The Sound of Silence" filled the ancient church, her eyes closed tight, her body becoming rigid as if in physical pain. I wanted her to stop, to stop the sorrow, to stop whatever memory this song brought her. She was like a mythical creature, her feelings echoed and felt by all who heard her music. I wanted her to stop, but the emotion was suffocating. I couldn't speak. Her face contorted as the tears came forth.

Finally there was silence, a deafening silence that echoed between the stone and glass, leaving a feeling of hopeless emptiness. Juliette fell into the arms of Sara, who hugged her so tight I wondered if Juliette was able to breathe. Jonah's arm and body were strong against my own. The pain of this moment was overwhelming.

I understood how much I did not know of the girl in front of me. She felt so deeply, she loved so deeply, she lost so deeply. She was the embodiment of beauty that was desperately needed in a world of darkness. I thought of her parents. Of how much they must have loved her. Not because of her abilities, but because she played for them. I could sense that. It was clear in a way few things were. I held onto Jonah as Sara held onto Juliette, each of them crying. Beside them, Sage rested her hand on her stomach, her eyes staring unseeing at the ceiling. Behind them Blaise walked away,

Josh following her. Behind us, Felicia sobbed as Richard held her.

Each of us lived in that same darkened world. Each of us made the choice to live or to die, to hope or to give up. I wondered about Juliette's mom and dad. Were they alive? She spoke once of her brother. Was he alive?

Juliette released Sara's shoulders and sniffed. She had lost so much, but she was strong. Stronger than any of us. I wondered if Haz had seen that. When he told her that her time was done, that this fight was not hers, had he seen her strength? Was he afraid, as I was, that she would want to enter the fight? She was young and, like Astrea, she followed our lead and did what we asked. That would not always be the case. Soon, very soon, she'd be grown and she'd understand the world better and … she would fight.

Eight
BRIA

I lay beside Jonah in a corner of the still church. Our friends had spread out among the pews and corners. Sara was on watch in the first row of the church; the others were asleep or falling asleep. This was the farthest away from any of them I had slept since I lay bleeding on the floor of Trent's apartment. I waited as that thought entered and left my mind. I expected there to be pain associated with the memory, but there wasn't. It felt long ago, though it was only months. So much had changed in those few months. I had changed so much; maybe that's why this memory no longer hurt me. Had I grown enough to leave it behind?

The moon must have been rising because the windows on the east side of the church were illuminated, their colors almost as vivid as they had been when we first came here and the sunlight sifted through them. I understood the meaning of some of the windows. The one with the serpent, apple, and two people was obvious, but the one closest to us was not. It showed a man that must have been Jesus, sitting on a stone circle, a woman with a large ceramic jug beside him, and sand at their feet. He had his hand open toward her, as if inviting her forward. I didn't recognize this story. JP would be able to tell me what it was about, and I wouldn't feel stupid asking him. He would like this church. He loved beauty and this church embodied that. My father had told me once, when I was young, that Catholics tried to lure people in with beauty. I didn't understand what he meant until now. Being here made me want to stay longer. It was peaceful and serene. The statues, the stained glass, even the stone floors—all beauty.

"You're so beautiful," Jonah said from beside me.

"That's funny, I was thinking the same thing," I said with a faint laugh.

"You were thinking how beautiful you were?" Jonah said in subtle surprise.

I laughed. "No, I was thinking of how beautiful this place is."

"It is," he said, "but the most beautiful thing God ever created was woman, and you are a particularly exquisite example of his artistry."

I grinned. "That is a lame pickup line."

He smiled half a smile. "I'm pretty sure we're past the pickup line stage," he said as his fingers traced my ear, sending a tingle through my body. "And I wasn't kidding. Nothing in the world compares to you."

I leaned into him, pressing my lips to his. His mouth softly parted to allow our kiss to deepen.

"Yeah, we are way past the pickup line," I said, still kissing him, my body pressed against his.

His hand was against the small of my back, pulling me closer. My left leg lifted and encircled his legs. My hand slid up the back of his shirt. He had given me the time I needed, the time to heal, to be ready for the next step in our relationship, and I was ready. I pulled him in tighter. I wanted all of him and I wanted to give him all of myself.

His back became rigid, his lips left mine, and he pushed himself away from me.

"What's wrong?" I asked, feeling hurt as he sat up, clearly signaling he wasn't interested.

He shook his head and held up a finger to tell me to wait. I sat beside him, my back against the stone wall of the church. I was trying hard not to allow the rejection I felt to turn to anger.

He opened his eyes. "I'm okay," he said. "I just wasn't … prepared for that." He was trying to slow his breathing.

"For what?"

"For the intense desire to forget everything that is good and true and …"—he shook his head as if to distract his thoughts—"and make a different choice."

"You don't want to be with me?" I asked, my voice sounding like that of a pouting child. I hated that, but it was better than lashing out.

"Bria, I can't begin to explain how badly I want you …"—he cleared his throat—"to be mine, but I can't. I mean I can. I mean,"—he paused, pinching the bridge of his nose—

71

"I mean I want to give myself to you totally and completely and that can't happen right now."

"But you said you were ready to go as slow or as fast as I wanted," I said, my hand touching his waist. "And I'm ready."

He jumped back, blocking my hand from his waist. "I so need a pile of snow or a thorn bush," he mumbled.

I tried not to be angry, but I couldn't help it. "What're you talking about?"

"Nothing," he said, shaking his head. "I'm not going to hook up with you."

"Hook up with me?" I said in full anger. "This is so not a hookup. We're in a committed relationship."

"We're not married."

"So, we love each other."

"So?"

"So that counts," I said, not believing I was having this conversation with a guy, any guy.

He scoffed and rolled his eyes.

"Seriously? You seriously just rolled your eyes at me?"

"You are being a typical guy," he said. "I figured I would be a typical girl."

I wanted to shout, but I kept my voice low. "What does that even mean?"

"It means you are totally trying to seduce me and I'm not having it," he said with a hint of amusement.

"I'm not … I'm not trying to seduce you," I said, doubting my own words.

"If you were the guy and I was the girl and you were doing and saying exactly what you are doing and saying, what would that be?" He folded his arms.

I bit my lip. "A lot of pressure," I said.

He nodded his head in triumph.

"I'm sorry, I … I've never been turned down before," I said, letting go of my anger.

"I'm going to ignore that statement. It implies there were guys before me and I don't like to think about that."

I hung my head.

He lifted my chin. "Forget I said that. The point is that sex means something more to me than it means to you, and if I had sex with you, it wouldn't be fair to either of us."

"Oh, I'm sure it would be more than fair," I said, teasing.

He shook his head.

"Okay, okay, I'm sorry," I said, making my expression as serious as I could.

"Besides," he said, "we're in a church. I mean, it doesn't get more wrong than that."

"God doesn't like sex?" My eyebrows pulled together in a way that I was sure looked ridiculous, but I didn't care.

"No, God loves sex," Jonah said.

The thought of that was weird and my face must have shown it.

Jonah shook his head. "What I meant to say is sex is designed to be the seal creating the physical bond that the marriage vows create in words. The two, sex and marriage, go together. Separating them is not part of God's plan and that means it won't lead us to happiness."

His words sounded rehearsed.

"Sex is a seal?" I asked, wondering how I had fallen in love with a man who was so good that he was actually willing to not sleep with me because of God, or something about God, or I didn't even know. None of this made sense, none of it except that I loved Jonah and I wanted to show him that.

He sat up straighter. "It's part of the marriage covenant. You offer your body, your life, to your spouse as part of that covenant."

He still sounded like he was reading from a book.

I crossed my arms and said, "I seriously have no idea what you're talking about and it sounds totally scripted."

"It's because I can't think clearly," he said, rubbing his temples with his hand.

"Take a minute, and then try to explain what you're trying to explain," I said, being as patient as possible.

He cleared his throat. "Okay, I know what to say," he said shyly.

I uncrossed my arms, trying to appear receptive to words that would likely make no sense.

He moved onto one knee and took my hand in his. "Will you marry me?"

"Will I what?"

"Will you marry me?" he repeated, with no hint of joking.

"Jonah, I love you. I really, really do, but I think you've lost your mind."

"See, that's just it," he said, as if proving his point.

"What is?"

"You think I'm crazy for asking you to marry me," he said in triumph.

"Yes, yes I do."

"But see, sex was designed to sort of do the same thing marriage does. It was meant to bond us together for life. So if you think the idea of marrying me sounds crazy, then the idea of having sex with me should also sound crazy."

"So ... you don't want me to marry you?" I asked, suddenly realizing he'd proposed to prove a point and it wasn't real.

He took my hand in his and sat beside me, our bodies facing one another.

"Bria, I am so in love with you," he said softly. "There is nothing I want more than to be the man you share your life with."

"Do you mean that or are you proving a point?" I said, feeling confused and a little hurt.

"I'm sorry if you thought I asked you to marry me to make my point. That was just a bonus," he said, teasing. His finger traced my jawline. "The proposal was one hundred percent real."

My expression was blank.

"You still don't believe me," he said as he rocked onto his knees. "Will you stand, please?" he asked, gently guiding me to my feet. He took my hand in his.

"Gabriella Marie Ford …"—his voice was loud, echoing throughout the church—"I love you. You are the most amazing woman I have ever met. I can't imagine my life without you and I don't want to. More than anything else I have ever wanted, I want to be yours. Will you please do me the honor of allowing me to be your husband?"

I knelt beside him. "More than anything else I've ever wanted, I want to be yours," I whispered, leaning toward him.

He wrapped his arms around my back.

"Wha'd she say?" Josh's voice called from across the church.

Jonah and I laughed as we held one another. Our bodies became unsteady, and I fell, tumbling on top of him.

"Yes," I yelled. "I said yes."

Cheers rang out across the church as our friends ran to us, surrounding us with hugs and congratulations. Juliette left us and ran to the piano, Astrea chasing her. Soon the church was charged with music. After Juliette played Pachelbel's *Canon*, she began a second, slower song.

Jonah stood. "Will you dance with me?" he asked, his hand outstretched toward me.

I took his hand. "Yes," I said.

How long had it been since I'd danced? Sara and I used to go to clubs when Trent was out of town or with his friends. We danced with whatever guy was around. It didn't mean anything to us or to them. Jonah's arm wrapped tenderly around my back. He held my left hand against his heart. He moved me gently to the music. This was different; this meant everything.

A pang of guilt ran through my heart.

***

Our friends slept. Jonah told Sara he would be on watch. He said he was too excited to sleep. My head rested on his shoulder, our backs against the stone.

The moon shifted or the clouds did, and the window containing Adam and Eve became illuminated. Fear entered my mind.

"Did you really understand what you were doing?" I asked, the words coming out before I could stop them.

"What I was doing?" Jonah asked, his voice full of tender devotion.

"When you asked me to marry you. I have baggage, a lot of baggage," I said, as images of past mistakes flashed through my mind.

"You remember I beat up my dad and spent eight months in jail?" he said.

"That's different," I said.

Jonah was silent. I lifted my head, wondering if he'd fallen asleep. But his eyes were alert. He was staring toward the crucifix. His arm tightened around my shoulder when he realized I was watching him.

He said softly, "I don't want someone who's never messed up. That person doesn't exist. What I want is for you to let me love you and for you to love me. I want a partner who will challenge me to be better and stand beside me when I'm not. I want to spend my life with you, striving toward holiness. I'm sure that sounds bizarre to you, but that's what our marriage will be for me."

I placed my hand on his chest and snuggled closer. "It doesn't sound bizarre. It does make me wonder if I'm the right person for you," I said, not wanting to say those words, yet having to at the same time.

He kissed my hair. "You are and you always will be. For me, this is for life."

And I could tell that part was something he was concerned about—not about him, but about me. He wondered if I believed the same.

"For me too," I whispered.

I'm not sure why, but I have always believed in marriage, always believed it was forever. I remembered how my parents were and how happy they had been. It was so long ago and I was so young, and I have seen so many awful marriages since then. But somehow that image stuck. The image of what it could be, and that was what I wanted.

"I love you," he whispered.

"I love you too."

In front of me: The image of Jesus on the stone circle, the woman beside him with a ceramic jug. A wooden pail at Jesus's feet. He was speaking to her, welcoming her. They were at a well. She was afraid and excited, or thirsty. I would have to remember to ask JP about that story, I thought, as I drifted to sleep.

Nine
EAST

Man-made light flooded the cave.

"Crouch down lower," John said.

We were huddled beside each other, behind the rock wall. Haz was asleep at our feet.

We were safe where we were; the light couldn't reach us. The only shadows against the far wall of the cave were of rocks. The helicopter was loud, hovering near the entrance to our cave. They were as near as they could come and not hit the long blades against the rocks. The beam of light bounced in and out as the pilot struggled to keep the helicopter steady. We couldn't be detected from where they hovered. If they wanted to search the cave properly, they'd have to climb up. I hoped they were too lazy. I hoped they would leave us alone ….

Gunfire shattered my thoughts. I threw myself on top of Haz, and John lay beside us. We covered our heads with our hands while bullets ricocheted like pinballs off the stone walls. I fought the urge to scream when something hit my back. I moved my hand; a jagged edge of broken rock lay on my spine. I exhaled, my head falling onto Haz's chest in relief. It was only a chunk of rock, not a bullet.

Haz opened his eyes, understanding flashed, and he forced his body above mine. The noise was deafening, making it difficult to think. His protective instincts were stronger than in anyone else I'd met. I admired him for that.

The gunshots stopped and the light faded. Haz pushed himself off my body, squatting and peering from behind the rock wall. Light faded into darkness. Noise faded into quiet.

I pushed myself into a sitting position and brushed the dirt from my body.

"I think they're gone," Haz said.

"Do you think they realized we're here?" John asked, his breathing ragged and scared.

It was too dark to see him, but his voice told me he was beside me.

Haz answered, "I'm sure they didn't."

"If they had, they would've made someone climb up here and flush us out—or try to," I said.

John said, "They were shooting for fun?"

"They were trying to flush us out, or kill us," Haz said. "Whichever one happened to work."

No one spoke for several minutes. My ears were still ringing from the sound of bullets exploding chunks of rock.

John asked, "What do we do?"

"You should try to sleep," I said. "You both should."

"Sleep?" John said. "We were just shot at."

I leaned my back against the damp wall. "Exactly. Shot at, not shot," I said.

"This time," John said.

"What do you want to do?" Haz asked.

I felt him extend his leg, probably the one that had been shot during the climb.

John moved in the darkness. "Get out of here. Run," he said.

"In other words," I said, "do exactly what they were trying to get us to do."

Haz offered a faint chuckle as he stretched his body to prepare for sleep. John did the opposite, pulling in his legs. He didn't feel safe, and I didn't blame him—but this was our reality. We had to appreciate peace, even if that peace came directly after being shot at.

"No, I guess we shouldn't run," John said after a while.

From beside him, Haz's breathing shifted. He had fallen asleep. It was good; he needed to sleep, but it concerned me that he fell asleep so easily. It typically took him longer. Though he did always fall asleep fastest when I was on watch. He trusted me and respected my ability to keep him safe. I felt the same about him.

"The electricity took a lot out of him," John said as if responding to my unspoken concern.

"Yes, it did," I said softly, praying Haz would be stronger tomorrow. I listened to his steady breathing and felt better. He would heal quickly. He always did.

In this dark cave, with our bodies touching, it was difficult to pretend we didn't have feelings for one another. I shook my head to clear away the thought. He and I wouldn't work. There were too many differences. We weren't even born in the same decade. I needed to focus on keeping us safe and getting us home, and he needed to focus on healing.

"Who are you?" John said quietly, so quiet I wasn't sure if he was talking to me or someone else, though there was no one else.

I turned my head toward his voice. "My name is East."

"I gathered that much," he said, in a way that told me he once laughed easily but now he didn't. "Why are you here? Why did you rescue us?"

"We're here to help and we rescued you because you needed to be rescued," I said.

"But why? It wasn't easy to reach us. How did you know we were there?"

His voice was skeptical; he didn't trust us. That actually made me like him more. It showed he had some sense of self-preservation, and I appreciated that.

"We came to Camp David because Haz, the man who's asleep between us, believed some prisoners had been taken there. We weren't sure how many or if any were still alive, so we thought we should find out."

"In the beginning, there were more of us," he said with hardness in his voice.

There had been so much loss, it was impossible to escape.

"I'm sorry for the others and for you," I said, "if they were people you were close to."

"I lost colleagues there. I cared about them as such. I mourned their deaths and pray for their souls, but their screams are not the ones that haunt my dreams," he said with such pain that I felt it within my own heart.

"Whose are?" I asked softly.

"Why did you save us?" John asked, the pain replaced by anger at my asking about those he loved most deeply.

"I'm sorry if that was too personal," I said. "We rescued you and the others because we're hoping you can help us."

"Help you? How?" he asked skeptically.

"By figuring out how to save the country."

He laughed a tired, angry laugh. I wished I could see his face to better understand what it meant. His actions made me uncomfortable. I held the pistol tighter.

"Of all the people on the planet, we are the very ones who could never help you."

His tone was angry, but it was directed at himself and those he had been with. He had not been their enemy, but he had not been their friend either. I didn't understand their relationships or how he was so certain they would be no help.

"Why is that? You said you worked together. What sort of work?" I asked, keeping my voice calm as my hand held the pistol and my ears listened for the slightest sound of him moving toward me. It was good he couldn't see how little I trusted him—though if I could see him, I might trust him more.

John laughed, again in anger. "I was a politician."

"The others with you were the same?" I asked, trying to understand why that mattered, why they could never help us, as he said.

I didn't care about politics. My dad told me I should, but I didn't. Politicians were all the same. They made promises they didn't keep. Did it matter which promises they made? Jonah and I used to fight about this. It was one among many things we fought about.

"The others were worse," he said. "They'd been there for decades, entrenched in the destruction."

"Where had they been?" I asked. I felt like he was speaking in code. Jonah would understand what he was talking about without asking. Haz probably would too, but I had no idea.

"Congress," he answered.

I should've paid more attention in school so I'd understand what sorts of things Congress controlled.

"What did you mean when you said they were entrenched in the destruction?" I asked.

"How much have you been told about what happened?" he asked.

"The country imploded, we destroyed ourselves."

This is what Haz told us had happened and it was supported by comments Trent made, and as sad as it was, it sounded plausible. Even someone who didn't pay attention to politics realized that civility had long ago left our government. Our politicians reminded me more of actors in a poorly written, overly dramatic play than they did of men and women working to make anything better.

John replied, "We did destroy ourselves, and we all need to take responsibility for that. But there are some who have more responsibility than others. Some made the decision to destroy our country and other countries along with it. It's on their consciences that the death of millions, or hundreds of millions, rests." His words were fueled by anger, but behind the anger was sad defeat.

"Who decided to do this?" I asked, my fingers tightening around the gun in my lap. Was he one of the people who had destroyed the world?

"There was no one person who caused this, but many were part of it and many more who, in their warped minds, led them to make that choice."

"Did you know them—the ones who were part of this?" I asked, keeping my voice calm. I held the pistol tight, ready.

For many seconds, John said nothing. The sound of gunfire rang in the distance.

"Derrick, the man I was with—the man you rescued—was one of the people who did this," he said, his voice sad.

"Did he tell you?" I asked. It was the only thought that came to my mind as I struggled to keep the scream of hatred inside me.

"I had no idea," he said, his voice breaking.

Ten
BRIA

Juliette sat at the piano, her fingers creating sounds that combined the beauty of heaven and the pain of earth.

"I wonder how she learned to play like that?" Sage asked as we gathered our supplies.

"I wonder a lot of things about her," Blaise said, opening the magazine of her pistol to double-check it was full.

"She's a mystery," Sara said.

Josh sifted through his pack. "I thought she talked to you," he said.

"She does, but never about her past," Sara said.

"Have you ever asked her about what happened to her family?" Jonah asked.

"How could I ask that?" Sara said, zipping her pack. "They must be dead, and to bring that up would be too painful."

"Her parents must've been nice," Sage said, in a thoughtful sort of way. "She's nice."

Blaise shoved the magazine back into the pistol, anger pouring out of her.

"Sorry," Sage said, when she realized her offense.

Blaise glared at Sage and stomped away to the back of the church. That level of anger, directed at one of us, wasn't what I expected from Blaise. Josh watched her go but did not follow her. This was not what I expected from him. Though I couldn't blame him. Blaise had been in an awful mood all morning.

I turned back toward the music. Richard and Felicia sat behind Juliette, his arm around his wife as a tear ran down her cheek. His eyes were on the crucifix that hung above the altar. Her gaze bounced from Juliette to Blaise to the crucifix.

"It's so graphic," I said.

"What is?" Jonah asked.

I nodded toward the crucified man.

"Totally," Josh said, shuddering at the sight of the crucifix.

"It's sort of difficult to believe in a God who was killed on a cross," I said, before I realized what I was saying and who I was saying it to.

"The ultimate humiliation," Jonah said, zipping his pack. My words had not offended him.

"Not all Christian churches have a crucifix," Josh said. "Most just have a cross."

Sara mumbled, "And some don't even have that."

I wondered if that made it better: not being able to see the dying man.

Jonah slipped his arms through the straps of his backpack. "Catholics are not a sugar-coating people. We tell it like it is. Good or bad, joy or pain."

"Even the windows are gruesome," I said, as I saw images of Jesus being beaten, whipped, spit upon, blood dripping into his eyes and mouth. "They're awful."

"The only way to the Resurrection is through the cross," Sara said. "To deny the suffering or sacrifice would be to deny what it was all about. He suffered and died for us, each of us. It was brutal, and it shouldn't be forgotten or dismissed or minimized."

I turned from the windows. "Why not?"

"Why not?" Jonah echoed.

"Yeah, why can't the images be less graphic? Why can't they focus more on happy times, like the Resurrection, instead of the Crucifixion?" I asked.

Jonah slid his pistol between his shirt and the waistband of his pants. "He didn't die because of happy times, he died because of the darkness we each bring into the world."

"Then why make the churches so beautiful?" Sage asked.

She was right. This church, with its gothic gruesomeness, called to me in a way that no man-made structure ever had.

"There's nothing more beautiful than a sacrifice freely given," Jonah said. "And Jesus's sacrifice for each of us is overwhelmingly beautiful. It's what inspired the artists of these windows and this church, and all the other sacred Christian art throughout the last two thousand years."

"Every ounce of beauty in the world is from God," Sara said, "but there's darkness too. Not from God, of course, but it exists and there's no point in denying it. Our lives currently—and, I guess, before, too—are an example of that."

Juliette's song stopped, and my heart cried out for more. How long would it be before I heard music again? Juliette ran her fingers along the polished wood, letting them rest as she closed her eyes. I wondered what was in her mind at that moment. Her hand flattened against the piano, as if in longing, then lifted as she turned and picked up her pack. Sara wrapped an arm around her and Juliette nuzzled into her chest. I realized that Sara had become something of a mother to Juliette. The realization made me mostly happy, though still, when I saw Juliette, I wondered so deeply about those who had created and raised her. She was a girl like no other. Her parents must be the same.

Richard and Felicia entered my line of sight and my thoughts changed. Blaise, too, was remarkable. Before, I would have said her parents were equally as remarkable. Now I understood they were deeply flawed. As flawed as I was, perhaps more. Jonah and Charlotte each had spoken about the choices we make. Was that the answer to how they became murderers? Maybe it was not that one person was immune to sin, while another entered into it without hesitation. Perhaps instead, it was that one person made a choice and another made a different choice, and over time those choices defined us. Richard and Felicia, before the light, chose to love. After the light they chose hate. They saw those working at the farm as the other. Someone less than them and, ultimately, someone who was not a person, but rather an object to be controlled by any means necessary.

Others had done the same. I remembered professors discussing the horrors of Auschwitz and Rwanda. Of our own country's disgusting history of slavery. I remembered the words Haz spoke in frustration at Josh's lack of understanding when Juliette first came to us. Slavery existed before and it still exists. I hadn't understood then that slavery still existed in the United States, but hearing Mrs. Pryce speak of Jazmyne, I understood it did. Was every person who committed such acts of evil, evil themselves? Were Felicia and Richard? Or could it be that any one of us could make such choices if, over time, we chose small acts of darkness?

The stained glass in front of me depicted another scene, one familiar to me. JP had gazed often at this same picture while I read him the accompanying story. In the window, Jesus emerged from a river, water dripping from his hair and body. Another man, John the Baptist, stood above him, and a white dove hovered above both of them. This was Jesus's baptism and it marked the beginning of his public life and ministry. His life had been slated more than the rest of ours, but Eli said even Jesus had a choice and even he was tempted.

I turned back to see the man from the life-giving river hanging on a cross. He had chosen that sacrifice. I understood that. I don't know how or why, but I did.

Jonah's hand slid into the white marble basin. At the bottom of the basin was all that remained of the holy water that once occupied it. He touched the water and lifted his fingers to his forehead, chest, and shoulders as he turned and knelt one last time in front of the man hanging on the cross. Jonah's expression was of longing and pain. He did not want to be separated from his Savior.

He rose and asked, "Are you all right?"

I blinked. The beauty of him, a man who consistently chose to do what he believed was right, rather than what he merely wanted to do, brought tears to my eyes. "You are beautiful," I said.

He wrapped an arm around my shoulders and kissed me on the side of my head. "You are too."

The doors behind me opened and morning light streamed in, illuminating the man on the cross. I bit my lip and made a choice. My right hand shook as I slid my fingers along the edge of the marble … to the thin film of liquid that covered the bottom. I closed my eyes, then opened them. With concentration, I lifted my fingers … first to my forehead … then to my chest … to the left shoulder … and to the right shoulder.

"You blessed yourself?" Jonah said in surprised confusion.

"I made a choice," I said, "to open my heart and mind to the possibility of more."

He held his hand open, and I slid my fingers into his as the crisp morning air chilled my lungs. The day was bright—not a cloud in the sky. We would be home in less than a week and our life together would begin. A new life, a new beginning.

Eleven
BRIA

I found myself wishing for shorts, but even if I had them I wouldn't wear them. I hadn't shaved since Blaise's wedding. It didn't matter if everything else was different—hairy legs were still hairy legs. I'd shave when we got home and try to find some shorts or dresses of my mom's. There it would be safe to wear shorts; we would not be fighting through the underbrush.

We hadn't seen or heard signs of the military since entering North Carolina. There were signs of other people and predators, but both in balance and neither came near us.

"How should we cross?" Josh asked.

It was a stream, nothing more. The water was rushing, and even in the heat of summer it would be freezing, but it held no danger.

Sage sat on the rocks and started to remove her shoes.

"Sage is right," Richard said as he and Felicia leaned on boulders and did the same.

The rest of us followed. We tucked our socks inside our shoes and tied the shoes around our necks. I lifted my pant legs, pulling them up above my knees. I brushed one of my legs with a dry hand. At least the blonde hair matched my pale legs.

I stumbled along, trying to stay steady as my feet twisted and turned on the stones. Jonah and I held hands when we waded across the stream. We turned at the sound of a splash. Blaise had slipped on a loose rock.

She groaned, grabbing her shoulder as she rose from the water.

"Did you hit your shoulder?" Josh asked as he helped her across.

"No, I'm fine," she said in anger, as her wet shirt changed from a dark gray to a dark red.

"You're bleeding," Josh said with fear.

"It's nothing," Blaise said. She attempted to take her shoes from him, but he held them from her reach.

Felicia came to Blaise. "Can I see your shoulder?"

"I'm fine. Give me my shoes," Blaise said, shielding her shoulder from her mom.

"Why are you sweating? The water is freezing," Josh said, staring at his wife's face.

He was right. Her face was covered in a thin layer of sweat and the coloring was off. How long had it been that way? How had I not noticed?

"I'm not sweating. Give me my shoes," she said, leaping toward him.

"Not till you show me your shoulder," Josh said, holding her shoes high in the air.

"Fine, I don't need them," she shouted. She was across the stream, on the rocky beach. She continued forward, into the woods.

I moved, blocking her body with mine. "You can't go in there without your shoes. Let him see your shoulder."

"No," she said, shoving me.

I stumbled, falling into Richard. He caught me and lifted me to my feet.

"What's going on with you?" Sara said, placing her hand on Blaise's shoulder to stop her.

Blaise cried out in pain and swung her fist at Sara. Sara jumped backward, dodging the blow.

Josh ran to block his wife. "Have you lost your mind!"

"What do you care?" she shouted, running toward him, aiming her head and shoulders like a battering ram.

Josh extended his arms, using them to soften her impact against him. He fell to the ground, Blaise crumbling on top of him. She opened her mouth as if to speak, but no words came.

Her face drained of color, taking on the appearance of waxed death. Her eyes fluttered as the jet-black irises lifted, rolling back, disappearing into her skull. Her breathing turned to deep grunts, as if her body was forcing air to come and go in a futile attempt to fill her lungs.

"Blaise, Blaise!" Josh shouted in panic as he moved her unconscious body away from him and onto the stones.

We ran to her.

"What's wrong, what's happening?" Sara asked as she lifted Blaise's head into her lap, protecting her from the hard stones.

Felicia pulled the knife from Blaise's sheath. Jonah reached his hand to stop her.

"Leave her," Richard ordered, with the force of a father.

Jonah hesitated before releasing Felicia's hand.

Felicia cut the shirt from Blaise's arm. The gunshot wound that had been barely a scratch was oozing a whitish-green liquid mixed with blood. Felicia's eyes grew wide with fear. She turned her head away, sucked in air, and turned back to her daughter. She rocked to her knees, bending and kissing her on the forehead. Her fingers touched her own lips, causing a worried expression to form as she rocked up to a standing position.

"We can't stay here in the open," Felicia said. "Josh, take her into the woods. Start a fire, I'll need boiled water."

Felicia spoke with the same authority and focus I had heard in Charlotte when one of her kids was sick.

"Richard, come with me. We need to find whatever healing plants we can," she said, her eyes already scanning the banks and trees for the herbal medicine she needed.

I ran to the trees. There was a clearing big enough for a fire and Blaise's sleeping body. Juliette was beside me as we cleared debris, stacking twigs and branches in a pile for the fire. Jonah and Josh carried Blaise and laid her in the clearing. Juliette and I continued to find dried twigs and brush for a fire, while Sara removed a pack of matches from her bag. After layering the loose material just right, she lit the match. Dead grasses immediately caught. She placed first one and then another tiny twig. They caught. She repeated the process, layering thicker and thicker twigs until the fire was burning well. Sage brought filled water bottles, as Jonah pulled the blackened pot from his bag. I ran to the stream bed and returned with three stones that could be used to hold the metal above the fire. Sage poured the water into the pot and returned to the stream for more water.

Josh rubbed his wife's feet.

"What's going on?" Blaise asked, her voice sounding drunk.

Josh opened his mouth to speak, but before he could, Blaise had passed out again.

"Blaise, Blaise," Josh said softly.

When she didn't answer, he focused on rubbing her feet, his tears falling onto his hands.

"Felicia can fix this," I said, more to myself than anyone else. "She knows how to heal, she can save Blaise." I was rambling, but I was so scared I wasn't sure what else to do. Blaise and Sara were the closest things to sisters I had ever had. I loved Blaise like I loved myself, and I was terrified. When Trent held my life, it was my life. If I had died, then I would be dead and whatever happens at death would've happened. But if Blaise died, I would still be alive and it would be in a world where she wasn't, and I couldn't handle that. I bit my lip and turned away from Josh. Whatever I was feeling, he was feeling more—so much more.

"Richard, put your herbs in the pot," Felicia said as she jogged toward us. She placed a leaf in her mouth, chewed it up, took out a wad of green goop and stuffed it into Blaise's shoulder.

She placed other leaves, flowers, and roots on the flat part of her pack.

"Has she woken up?" Richard asked, gazing at his daughter.

"Only for a second," Sara responded.

We waited as the water boiled, and she threw all the herbs she'd collected into the pot. The smell of wild garlic was overpowering. No one spoke. Jonah knelt above Blaise, the palms of his hands extended toward her, his lips moving silently in prayer.

I closed my eyes. From somewhere deep inside, I allowed myself to pray for Blaise to get better.

Felicia removed the pot from the fire and swirled the contents over and over to cool them.

"Take this," she said, handing me a strip of cloth. "Wet it in the stream. We need to bring her fever down."

I did as I was told. The water was cold against my hand, forcing me to focus on the feeling instead of Blaise lying unconscious.

When I returned to the clearing, she was awake. Her mom was holding a bowl of tea to her lips. She sipped it. Her eyes were unfocused, her skin was without color and wet with perspiration. I handed the damp rag to Josh. He wiped the sweat from her forehead. She grimaced, pulling her legs up toward her as if she were cold. She closed her eyes.

"Richard, pour the liquid into this," Felicia said, handing him a bottle. "Keep the garlic and calendula chunks for a poultice."

Once the pot was empty, she poured the rest of the stream water into the pot and put it back on the makeshift stove.

"We need to clean the wound," she said with fearful anticipation.

I grimaced and turned my head at the thought. Cleaning a wound like the one Blaise had meant scraping it clean, ridding it of the pus and infection.

No one spoke as we waited for the water to boil again. Felicia dipped a rag into the water, using a stick to swirl it around and pull it back out. After allowing the rag to cool, she took it in her hand. She closed her eyes and opened them with resolve.

"Hold her," she said to Richard, barely breaking the silence.

Though he appeared startled by his wife's command, he placed his hands on Blaise's collarbone.

"What are you going to do?" Josh asked, his voice shaking. He had been so focused on Blaise, on soothing her, he must not have realized what Felicia was about to do.

"I have to pull the infection out," she said with determination, as her hand moved swiftly to the wound and scrubbed.

I bit my lip and turned away.

Blaise woke, screaming, reaching for her shoulder.

Josh cried as his wife screamed out in pain. He held her hand down and told her it was going to be okay, but I could barely understand the words, he was crying so much. Jonah came beside him and helped Richard hold Blaise. She writhed in pain, screaming and cursing. She began to kick. I grabbed one leg and Sara held the other.

In the distance, Juliette buried her face into Sage's chest. Sage turned her own face away and held tight to Astrea's collar. Astrea whined as she attempted to reach us. I wondered what she thought. She loved all of us. In the dog's mind, were we hurting Blaise?

Felicia dropped the rag as fresh red blood poured from the wound. She lifted the cooked herbs and packed them into the wound.

After doing this, she fell back, moving from the reach of her flailing daughter. I locked eyes with Sara. She nodded, and we released Blaise's legs and moved out of their reach. Jonah did the same with her arms, and then Richard. The only one who remained was Josh.

Blaise swung a fist. It connected with Josh's jaw. Hatred flashed in her eyes. He did not move. Her body calmed and her eyes closed. He sobbed quietly as he lifted a hand to his jaw. It was already swelling. He bent his head to hers, kissing her softly on the forehead.

Her eyes opened. "I love you," she whispered, and took his hand in hers and fell asleep.

I turned, not able to stop my tears. Their love and their pain were too much. Jonah wrapped his arms around me. I felt his chest rising and falling as he cried with me.

In sickness and in health: those words were repeating in my mind. Even when Blaise didn't recognize who Josh was. Even when she was fighting him in the angry imaginings of her delirious mind—he loved her, he took care of her. He sacrificed his well-being for hers. And she would do no less for him. This was marriage. It wasn't about getting; it was about giving. It was about sacrifice. It was about love, real love, not a fantasized version of it. He would love her and sacrifice for her until his dying day.

Sluggishly, Felicia got to her feet. Richard went to her and held her as she cried. She sniffed once and released him, not allowing herself to cry any more.

"Plantain must be here somewhere," she muttered. Her eyes scanned the nearby vegetation. "It's so common, how am I not seeing it?"

She went toward the trees.

Sara called out to her, "Maybe we have some."

"It must be here somewhere," Felicia said, not hearing Sara, still checking the plants around us.

Sara went to her discarded pack. "Blaise took some containers from your house. We split them up among our packs. I still have the ones she gave me."

"We do too," I said as Jonah retrieved our packs.

Felicia came to us and watched us pull her glass jars from socks at the bottom of our bags.

Her eyes grew wide. She took two of the jars from Jonah. The leaves within them were flat and brown. "I could kiss you," she said. "I could kiss each of you!"

Felicia opened the jars as she went to Blaise. "I'll need to clean her arm again and place these on the wound," she said.

Josh leaned over Blaise as if to protect her. "No, you can't. Let her sleep," he said.

Jonah went to him. "Her mom understands this stuff. It's the only chance Blaise has."

At first, Josh didn't move. Slowly he lifted his body from Blaise and turned his head, not wanting to witness the scrubbing that was about to take place.

Felicia boiled another rag and rapidly scrubbed the wound. Blaise screamed and thrashed, her eyes popping open as more blood appeared. Felicia dipped leaves into the boiling water, careful to keep her fingers from being burned. She held the leaves in the air and then laid them on Blaise's shoulder. Blaise writhed and cursed in pain.

It was the cursing that scared me the most. Blaise never cursed and hated when I did. How high was her fever? How long had this infection been growing without her telling any of us? Why was she so stubborn?

Felicia had finished with the wound. She backed out of her daughter's reach as Blaise's arm slipped from Josh's control. Felicia dodged the swing and stood beside her husband. Blaise's eyes fluttered shut. She was exhausted. Her body had woken only to fight the perceived attack.

"The dried leaves will buy us time while we search for the plant," Felicia said to Richard.

"What's going to happen to her?" It was the question we all wanted to ask, but only Sage was bold enough to do so.

Felicia slipped down to the ground, her face full of worry. She turned to Sage. "We'll know soon."

"What do you mean?" Josh asked, his voice cracking with fear.

In frustration, Felicia ran her fingers through her gray hair. Richard sat on the ground beside her.

"You know what that means, Josh," she said in anger. "This is the deciding moment of our daughter's life. Either the plantain will draw out the infection and she will survive the next few hours, or they won't and she won't."

The harsh bluntness hit me so hard it was difficult to see.

Josh stared in shock at Felicia's words.

"Were you aware of this infection?" Richard asked, accusing Josh of helping Blaise hide her secret.

He shook his head. "I should've realized," he mumbled. "I should've realized."

Twelve
EAST

By morning the guns had stopped, though the helicopters were back. Three of them circled the forest that surrounded Camp David. The dogs were on the ground, barking sporadically.

John was asleep. Haz had drifted in and out of sleep throughout the night. I didn't sleep and I wouldn't have, even if I hadn't been on watch. We helped a murderer escape from Camp David. That was not an easy truth to reconcile. No, Derrick did not pull a trigger and kill anyone, but his actions had led to the death of hundreds of millions of people, and we freed him.

Haz stirred as he woke. Dogs barked. John lifted his head with a jerk. He stared around the cave, trying to understand where he was. His sleep had been troubled, no bit of it peaceful. Light streamed into the main part of the cave. The tiny offshoot where we sat was growing brighter as the sun was crossing the treetops, aligning with our refuge.

As awareness took over, John lowered himself back to the rock floor.

Haz scooted beside me. "Did you sleep?"

I shook my head.

"I'm sorry," he said. "I should've stayed awake, but I was so tired."

"You got electrocuted, remember?"

Haz stared at me for a minute. "You're right. I thought that was a dream."

"Definitely not a dream," I said, wanting to laugh but too tired to do so.

"Man, that was a bad day," he said, rubbing his hair.

"And yet, not your worst one," I said.

He thought for a moment. "Not even close to the worst."

I leaned back against the cave wall. "I'm glad you're doing better."

"Me too. Now get some sleep. I'll be on watch."

I felt the heavy fatigue of sleeplessness, but the thoughts of what we had done wouldn't leave my mind.

"There's something you need to be told," I said.

"What?" he asked with tired concern.

"You were right. The older guy was a senator, and so was John." I nodded toward John, who had fallen back to sleep.

"I was fairly certain of that already," Haz said.

I paused when Haz looked at me expectantly. I swallowed hard. "The other guy, Derrick, he was one of the ones who did this," I said, pushing myself to say the words.

"Did this?" Haz asked with furious understanding.

I nodded.

"And we set him free?" he said, the rage and regret building.

I hung my head.

"Was he part of it?" Haz asked, his voice low and deadly as he gestured to John.

"He said we were all part of it. But no, he had no idea Derrick and the others were planning to blow up the world."

"You believed him?" he asked through gritted teeth.

"Yes," I answered. "He had nothing to do with it. I'm sure of it."

We sat. I stared at him. He stared at John.

"What do we do?" he finally asked.

"You're older and wiser. I was counting on you to tell me," I said, only partially joking.

He was both of those things, and as thoughts swirled in my brain all night, the only solution I could come up with was hoping that he'd devise a plan.

"I'm older, but definitely not wiser, and I have no idea what to do," he said.

He wasn't normally so vulnerably honest.

"What else did he say?" Haz asked.

"Nothing. After that, I was afraid if he said anything more, I might not be able to stay calm, and I didn't want to give away our position."

"You were afraid you were going to shoot him?" Haz asked with surprise.

"I didn't want to. That's why I didn't ask him anything else," I said, allowing myself to smile a bit.

"Thanks for not *wanting* to shoot me," John said, lifting himself into a sitting position.

"I hadn't meant for you to hear that," I said, my expression turning severe.

"You have every reason to want to shoot me. You wouldn't be the first. I doubt you'll be the last," he said, pushing his hair out of his eyes.

I wondered what he had looked like before the light. I doubted his hair had been long or his eyes defined by pain. Had I been able to see them last night, I wouldn't have been tempted to shoot him.

"Who else wanted to kill you?" Haz asked.

The echoes of bullets hitting trees and rocks in the valley filled the cave. A moment later the gunfire stopped. A minute or two after that, it started again. The shots were nowhere near where our friends had gone. John watched us to see if the gunfire bothered us. When he saw it didn't, he spoke.

"When I arrived at Camp David, there were twenty-three others. Some got sick or injured and died on their own, some starved themselves to death, but others were shot."

I asked, "Had they worked with Derrick to plan this?"

John shook his head. "The ones who planned this lived, at least for a while. Sometime in January, leadership changed and then … we were the only three left."

"Why did they allow you three to live?" I asked.

"I'm not sure. Derrick still had enough power to keep us alive, I guess."

Haz shifted, straightening his injured leg. "Why did he want you two alive?" he asked.

"He viewed me as his friend and he was adamant that Pam needed to live."

"Were you his friend?" I asked, glad I could see his eyes and whether or not he was telling the truth.

"I was kind to him when others weren't, but no, I did not count him as a friend."

"What about Pam?" Haz asked.

"They hated each other, but they had both been in DC for decades, so he was attached to her even though he couldn't stand her. To be honest, I have no idea why he fought so hard to keep her alive. But I never understood his mind. Not before and certainly not after."

"You told East he wasn't alone in doing this," Haz said, not bothering to hide his hatred for the old senator.

John shifted. He didn't like discussing this. "He was one of many, from different countries."

"Different countries?" I asked.

John nodded. "From what Derrick said, there were people from all the major developed nations in the world, who were working to cripple their nations."

"Why would anyone do that?" I said.

"They all had different lies they believed. Lies they fed to each other. Derrick's was that this was needed to give the US a new birth."

"That's disgusting," I said, the repulsion burning my throat. "How could anyone believe murdering innocents would help our country?" I said, trying to control the rage within me.

John rolled a pebble in his hand. "Things were messed up," he said thoughtfully. "That was obvious to everyone—but once I was elected and experienced it first hand,"—he allowed the pebble to roll from his palm—"I wasn't prepared for the level of dysfunction that existed in DC. Derrick believed this would fix it."

"He thought killing hundreds of millions of people would make things better?" Haz asked in angry disgust.

"I have to believe he didn't realize how many would die," John said.

"Lying to yourself won't help anything," Haz said. "I met Derrick. He could speak and think, which means he understood that people would freeze and starve. Planes would crash, surgeons would suddenly be operating in the dark with sources of oxygen and blood cut off from their patients. He would have known all of that, and he still made the active choice to kill all those people and the hundreds of millions more who have died since—and now those who are being targeted for death for no reason other than age or disability."

"You're right," John said, his face hot with pain. "All of this is based on lies. I can offer no excuses for him. He certainly offered none to me when they were ripping me from my family."

I allowed my back to fall against the cave wall. This was not his fault. He had lost as much as everyone else had.

"What happened to them?" I asked softly.

He stared past me, into the gray stone. "A helicopter came a few days after the attack. It landed on the roof of our building. Soldiers came to our door. My son Johnny opened it. He shouldn't have, but he didn't realize not to. They would have broken it down anyway," he said with accepted defeat. "They were going door to door. Many elected officials lived in our building. They were collecting us. I tried to fight them, but they pointed their guns at my wife and kids." He took a breath to slow his pain. "I stopped fighting and did what they said. They forced me up the stairs, to the roof. Derrick was there. He was sorry for me. I hated him then and every moment since then. Pam was also there, terrified. She was covered in blood. It was her husband's. They'd shot him as he tried to protect her. They loaded us up like the cowards we were and took us away."

John paused, picked up a handful of gravel, and let it slip slowly from his folded hand. "I can still hear my son screaming for me from the balcony. My wife was trying to pull him back inside and my daughter was standing, silent, behind them."

His voice was flat. His thumb looped tightly over the gold band on his left hand. He had once felt deeply; he had loved and been loved. That part of him was gone. He had done what he needed to do to survive, and what he needed was to stop feeling.

Thirteen
BRIA

Every time Blaise awoke, Josh forced her to drink the bitter tea of garlic and calendula her mother had prepared. Blaise spit it out the first time. The second time, Josh held her mouth closed until she swallowed it. When she was awake, her mind faded in and out of awareness. When she was asleep, her breathing was deep and labored. We covered her body in stream-chilled rags. Her arms, legs, forehead, stomach—everything we could—to help bring down the fever that was burning her mind, turning her brain to a garbled mess.

Jonah and Sage patrolled the area. Our tiny clearing offered no protection. Moving Blaise was too dangerous to her, but it didn't matter. We wouldn't be here long. Either she would live through the night or she wouldn't. Regardless, we'd be moving in the morning.

I tried not to think like that. I tried not to accept that my friend might die, but it was the truth and I couldn't deny it.

After searching for several hours, Felicia and Richard returned with stacks of broad green plantain leaves. Sara had been replacing the dried leaves every hour while they were gone. When the old leaves were pulled off Blaise, they were covered in brown slime and they smelled of disease. When Sara threw them into the fire, a putrid smell saturated the air.

"It's working," Felicia said, tracing the red lines that were running down Blaise's arm and chest. "These are getting shorter."

She crumbled a few of the dried leaves and put them into the herbal tea for Blaise to drink. We sat in silence, watching Blaise, while the sun began to fall back toward the earth.

Sometime not long after nightfall, Blaise woke. "Thank you," she whispered. She took a sip of tea and fell back asleep.

"Her fever must be getting better," Josh said with hope.

Felicia nodded, her tired eyes dark in the shadow of the firelight.

She removed all the rags except the one on Blaise's forehead, which she dampened and returned to the same area.

Blaise curled her body to a comfortable position.

Juliette was beside Sara and me. "Do you think she'll live?" she whispered so only the three of us could hear.

Sara returned the whisper. "Yes, I think so."

Juliette said "Thank you" into the night and laid her head and chest on Astrea. Seconds later, she was asleep, and Astrea, in turn, lowered her head and lay perfectly still so as not to disturb her master.

In sickness and in health. Those words continued to swirl in my mind as I watched Josh caress Blaise's hair, soaking wet from the stream water that had been applied throughout the day. Like Astrea, Josh kept his body still. My back and legs tightened at the thought of being stuck in the same position for so many hours. He didn't seem to mind. He was there for her. That was his purpose.

"It's beautiful, isn't it?" Sara said softly, her gaze following mine. "Their love is so true, so pure. It's the stuff of fairy tales, except it's real."

"It is," I said, nodding in agreement, hoping this fairy tale would have a happy ending.

"It's like you and Jonah," Sara said. "You two love each other just as much. He would care for you like Josh is taking care of Blaise."

As I watched Josh do all he could to keep Blaise alive, the thought of entwining my life with Jonah's brought fear. Life was so uncertain and marriage meant that instead of being uncertain about only my own life, I'd become uncertain about Jonah's life too. I glanced at where Sage stood, the profile of her belly a little rounder than it had been a week ago, and my fear deepened. What if we had a child? What if I died, like my mother had? What if the child died?

I loved JP and Quinn. The thought of something bad happening to them brought terror and panic and sent my mind swirling in pain, and they weren't even my children. Yes, I had aborted my first child, but I would never again wish death on a child of mine. I would love it in a way I had never felt love before. I saw that in Charlotte and Quint, Nonie and Pops, even in East. The death of a child—of Jonah's child—would be too much, and yet death was certain. Not necessarily at this moment, but soon. Nonie was the oldest this world would see for a long, long time. It was unlikely I would live to my father's age and even less likely Jonah would. How soon after our marriage would he leave me? How soon would I be a widow? Would I be like Jael, a widow before our first anniversary? Or would Jonah be left alone?

"Bria?" Sara said, her voice concerned.

I tried to slow my mind, telling myself I was tired. I wasn't thinking clearly because my best friend was on the brink of death. But it wouldn't slow; the panic was too strong, my thoughts jumping from fear to fear, from pain to pain.

The nervous energy forced me to stand. "I can't," I said as Sara watched me walk away.

I went to Jonah. His eyes held the same expression of concern that Sara's had.

"I can't," I said, my voice shaking. "I can't marry you."

His eyebrows pulled down in confusion. "Why?" he asked, his voice cracking.

"It doesn't matter, not really. I just can't."

I left the campsite and entered the woods. My mind continued to spin, nothing making sense. The image of Charlotte entered my mind. I wished I could talk to her, tell her how I was feeling. She would agree with me. She loved so deeply and that caused her so much pain. My mom's death, East's rape, our leaving—Charlotte had experienced pain.

This way was better. It was better not to love that deeply, to live without anyone. Eventually everyone would die. And I was not strong enough to handle that. I was not strong enough to hold Jonah's head as he barely clung to life—not again—now that I loved him completely. His death would kill me and, in this world, death was the only certain thing.

***

How fast life could change. You'd think I would understand that. You'd think everyone would understand it. Twenty-four hours ago I was engaged to the man I loved. Now I was alone. One best friend wouldn't speak to me and another was barely conscious. Jonah did his best not to look at me since I'd returned from the tree I'd slept in—or didn't sleep in. His eyes were red and swollen. It was better this way. It had to be. This had to be less pain than I would experience if we got married and then one of us died, which was bound to happen.

I needed something to do. I hated sitting here.

"Josh, can I take over for you?" He hadn't moved in a day.

"Take over for me?"

"I could take care of Blaise while you take a break or go for a walk or something."

"No, thanks," he said. "There's nowhere else I'd rather be."

I must have had a funny expression on my face, because he had a funny expression on his face and I assumed it was to match mine. "Taking care of her is a privilege and my right as her husband. I would never trade it even for a second."

I lowered myself, sitting beside him. Blaise's coloring and wound were improving. Her fever was down. She was out of the worst of the dangers.

"Are you scared?" I asked, aware I shouldn't say such a thing, not while his wife was still fighting for her life, but I couldn't stop myself.

"What do you mean?" he asked.

"If she dies."

His expression flashed five emotions at once. He was angry and hurt that I would ask such a thing, terrified I knew something he didn't, confused, and then understanding.

"Bria, I would never let fear keep me from Blaise. She was the woman I was made to spend my life with and only God knows how long that life will be. I'm not going to waste any of it being away from her. I realized soon after we met that she was the one I was meant to share my life with. That feeling all those months—or, I guess, years ago—totally freaked me out. Part of me wanted to run away from it, it was

122

so intense. But what if I'd given in to that fear? Where would I be? Someone else would be here with her. Someone else would be holding her and taking care of her. I would be the one missing out. If she dies, the best part of me will die with her, but I would rather live and die than never live."

I pulled myself away from him. I settled my back against a tree, pulled my knees to my chest, and wrapped my arms around them.

I sat there, for minutes or hours. The swirling fears gradually were replaced by the awareness of how stupid I'd been. The rest of the camp was changing around me. Blaise was sitting, fully awake, fully alive. I half listened as she spoke to her mom, thanking her for caring for her, the anger of two days ago replaced by the kindness I was used to. Josh kept a hand on her and she would have it no other way. Sara and Sage brought her food. Astrea crawled to her lap to be petted. Jonah, too, expressed how thankful he was that prayers had been answered. I alone said nothing. I should've been thinking of her, but I thought only of myself. Just as last night I'd thought only of myself.

It was time to move. Packs were ready. Josh helped Blaise stand. Richard and Jonah scattered the cold remains of the fire, doing what they could to cover the fact that we had been there. If someone came across this camp within a day, there would be no hiding our presence; in a few days, the grasses would lift and the clearing's memory of us would fade.

"Are you ready?" Jonah asked.

I lifted my eyes in hope. He was talking to Blaise and Josh, not me.

"Yes," Josh answered, "but we need to go slow. I don't think she'll make even half a day."

Jonah helped Blaise stand. "That's all right. Even a few miles would be helpful," Jonah answered.

Minutes later we were again moving toward home, Jonah taking the lead. Richard and Felicia stayed close to Blaise and Josh, the four of them walking in a small pack, their relationships beginning to heal at a level that Blaise and Josh had not been ready to accept before.

I was beside Sage, who was unaware of the broken engagement and of my selfish stupidity. She was too engrossed in her own challenges to think of others. Juliette, however, was more observant.

"Why aren't you with Jonah?" she asked as we stopped to allow Blaise to rest.

She must have realized we'd broken up. Of course she had; she wasn't stupid. What could I say to her? Though only a child, she was wiser than me. Why had I broken up with him? Fear. That was the answer.

"To spend your life with someone, especially with the world the way it is, it's terrifying," I said, trying to sound less crazy than I was.

"It is terrifying," she said softly, "but I meant, why aren't you physically walking beside Jonah?"

My face turned crimson.

Before I could think of a reply, she said, "Life is hard and it has always been hard. My parents loved each other,"—her voice choked—"their marriage was not always easy, but they made the commitment to face life together, no matter how scary life got. That's how they were, even until"—she paused and, with determination, said—"they could no longer be together."

"What happened to them?" I asked, the thought blurting out. It amazed me that I had any friends at all. I was selfish and mean and I asked questions a person should never ask. "I'm sorry, I didn't mean to say that out loud," I said.

"It's … it's okay."

She wanted to hide from the memories. I could hear it in her voice. But she didn't hide.

"My father was taken. My mother was killed … trying to protect my brother and me."

She forced the tears back. "Don't throw away the greatest gift you've ever been given because you're afraid. Even you are not that much of a coward."

The words stung. They were true. I was a coward. So much of my life, of my choices in life, had been made out of fear or complacency. I had time and time again allowed others to make choices for me. When had I ever fought for what I believed in? When had I ever truly known what that even was?

"Thank you," I said, and sprinted to Jonah.

"Hey," I said.

He didn't turn to face me. "What?" he asked.

His tone was callous and uncaring. I wanted to run, but didn't. "I'm sorry. I got freaked out, watching Blaise practically die, and I'm sorry."

"You don't need to apologize," he said, anger dripping from every word.

"But … I-I do. I do need to apologize. I messed up. I didn't mean it. I love you. I want to marry you and I'm sorry. I'm really sorry."

"This is not the time." His words were quieter but no less angry.

"Why … why not?" I said, a soul-crushing fear overwhelming me. Making me realize how badly I had messed up.

He said nothing.

"Jonah, please," I begged, touching his arm.

At my touch he softened, and then recoiled, shaking my hand off. My lungs constricted; I could barely breathe.

Still nothing.

"Please, please talk to me." *Please forgive me,* I prayed.

"Not now," he said in a hissing whisper. "Not in front of everyone."

I had forgotten the others were behind us. I turned. They were all staring at us. I didn't care.

"It doesn't matter. It doesn't matter what they think. I messed up. I was scared and impulsive and selfish. I love you. I want more than anything to be your wife. Please, please forgive me."

"You don't even know what it means," he snapped, no longer trying to hide his anger or keep the conversation private.

"What it means?" I asked, trying not to upset him, but unable to understand.

"To be someone's wife," he said in frustration. "To be married. You don't even understand what that means. I was stupid to think you did. How could you?" he said, shaking his head.

"I-I do know what it means, and I'll be a good wife," I said, my voice weak. I hated that.

"Ha! At the first sign of anything of concern, what did you do? As your friend was dying, what did you do? You bailed! You shoved me away!"

He glared at me. The skin around his eyes was red and swollen. He had been crying, but the tears were gone and in their place I saw no sadness, only anger. I'd hurt him and my heart broke.

"Shoving me out is not marriage. That is not even a healthy dating relationship. You have no clue how to do this."

Fury ... I felt fury rising, taking over. I would not lose him. I would fight.

"No, no, no," I screamed. "How dare you!" Tears of anger streamed down my face. I whirled, pushing him back against a tree. "Did your mom die? Did your dad abandon you? Did he take away your God? Did your first real relationship end in death? Did you ever feel so awful about yourself that you purposefully allowed yourself to be told repeatedly that you were worthless because you believed with every cell in your body you were, in fact, worthless? Did the person who said they loved you and wanted to marry you beat you so bad that you lay bleeding and unconscious on the bedroom floor? Did you get hunted down, and then you had to kill?" I screamed, my rage unrelenting. "You knew all of that, every failed piece of my failed life and still you fell in love with me and still you proposed, and so, yeah, I freaked out last night. That's going to happen. Is it fair to you? Probably not, but I'm broken and I've never hidden that from you. I promise you I will never leave again." I calmed my voice. "I hurt you and I'm sorry. I'm so sorry, but don't pretend like you didn't know exactly what you were getting into. I'm wounded. But I am in this. Yes, you are going to have to help me. Yes, there are going to be times when I lose it, but I'm here and I'm never leaving again. Till death do us part. I am yours, you are mine."

"It hurt," he said, the whites of his eyes growing red. "It hurt when you said you couldn't marry me. It hurt when you walked away from me and didn't talk and didn't even try to explain what you were feeling. You simply pushed me away. It reminded me of that first night at your grandparents' house. That rejection took me months to get over. I can't go through that again," he said, his eyes locked on mine.

"I'm sorry. I'm so sorry," I said, reaching my hand toward his.

He allowed me to take his hand. His grip was even tighter than mine. I pressed against his chest. His head rested on mine and he wrapped his arms around me.

"Nothing in this world can hurt me as much as you leaving," he said.

I lifted my eyes to his. "That's why I freaked out. I thought about you, lying there, instead of Blaise."

"Someday we will die," he said, his arms holding me tight. "We have no control over that. We only control how we live, and I choose to live focused on love, not fear."

"Fear can be so overpowering," I said, my arms clinging to him like I was a child.

"Don't you see? That's why we have each other. Love isn't only for when it's easy and fun. It's for the times when we're being crushed by fear or beaten down by despair. Those are the times we have to cling to one another."

"Will you help me?" I asked. "When my mind is swirling and I can't think, will you help me?"

"Bria, I will be beside you every moment you allow me to be beside you. But you have to let me in."

I tightened my arms around him, pushing my body against his. He hugged me, and for the first time in a long time, I felt safe.

Fourteen
EAST

We tied a rope to a rock at the top of the cave. I was the fastest climber, so I went down first … followed by John and Haz. There was no way to retrieve or hide the rope, but it didn't matter. We were no longer in the cave.

We were in the trees, going toward our town. We'd avoid the routes our friends would be taking and instead chose the most northern route. It would take us longer than the others, but that didn't matter. Haz had recovered and was back to his normal self, so we could go as far out of the way as we needed to and we'd still not be more than a day or two behind them. As it was, we should be in town in a day and a half, maybe less.

I was thankful yet again that Jael had told John to come with us. He was in good shape. Not as good as Haz and me, but for someone who had been a prisoner for seven months, he did well. He fought hard to keep up with us, and we only had to slow our pace moderately. We continued through the day and night. It had been my idea. The moon was full. A few more hours and we'd be home. We could sleep then.

We sprinted across the open field and asphalt dotted with what had once been cars—now nothing but a few unusable rusting parts. My legs ached as we climbed the familiar hill, but I didn't care. Halfway up, we tripped the wires. Even in the full moon, the wires were difficult to see. Metal clanged, and my body tensed with the awareness that HoneyBee and Jasper would soon be bounding toward us—if everything was okay in town.

We trudged forward. My fear at seeing the dogs was replaced by a more ominous fear of not seeing the dogs. That would mean the town had fallen or that our friends had fled.

Haz put an arm out to slow John.

Cautiously, we continued as the sound of running came from above us: heavy feet crashing through the trees and shrubs.

"Get back," Haz whispered, and we each moved behind a tree.

Haz peered from the side of his tree. My elbows were at my side, my hands up with the gun between them, ready to fire.

Haz's face brightened as he stepped from the tree. I turned my body, making it ready to fire if I needed to.

"Hey, Jasp," Haz called out as Jasper ran to him. Haz's arms circled the dog.

I lowered the gun as Jasper's master, Gus, broke through the bushes.

"Man, it is good to see you!" Gus said. "It's okay, y'all," he called up the mountain. "East and Haz are back."

Cheers rang out above us.

Jasper ran toward me as Gus embraced Haz. I jumped out of the way when Jasper tried to rub against me.

Haz and Gus chuckled.

"You don't like dogs, do you?" John said from beside me.

"Nope," Gus said, with a teasing wink, "she don't like dogs and she don't like hugs."

"I like hugs," I said.

"Uh-huh, sure you do," Gus teased.

"I do," I said, and I did—just not from men I'd known only a few weeks.

"How's everything at the town?" Haz asked, his hand on Gus's back.

"Real good," Gus said. "Crops are good, no one's sick."

"I guess that's all we can ask for these days," Haz said.

"Shoot, that's all we could ever ask for," Gus said. "Who's your friend?"

"John," John said, extending his right hand.

"Nice to meet you, sir. My name's Gus."

The two shook hands as Jasper wove in between them.

"What's his name?" John asked, petting the dog.

"Jasper," Gus replied. "And up above you'll meet his mate, HoneyBee, and four of their five pups, which ain't really pups no more. They've gotten even bigger since y'all left."

"Did the fifth one die?" John asked solemnly.

133

"No, no," Gus said. "We gave her to a girl traveling with her brother." He nodded to me.

My heart ached as I thought of Juliette and my friends. I asked, "Are the others back?"

"Nope. Y'all are the first," Gus said, attempting to sound unworried.

"We pushed pretty hard the last few hours," Haz said. "I'm sure they'll be here soon."

He was right. We had pushed hard. The other prisoners couldn't have kept up. They would probably be here when I awoke.

My body felt every mile and every minute of missed sleep as we started upward toward the town.

When we arrived, the lack of sleep was too strong to fight. A few people were around and were excited to see me, but their faces were blurry. My eyes were too exhausted to focus. I did my best to be polite before I went to the hut I shared with Becca.

I wondered if I should wake her and tell her I was back. I didn't have the strength. I crawled between my blankets and was asleep in an instant.

***

Everything in town was as it should be. Kids were playing and doing chores. Adults were talking and doing different chores. Everyone was working together for survival. Momma Pryce, as she insisted I call her, was first to greet me. I'd been too exhausted to speak to her last night, though she'd been waiting for us. Worried, I'm sure, every minute we were gone. She worried more than most and she loved more than most. She looked nothing like my grandmother and had lived a life nothing like she had lived, but still, Momma Pryce reminded me of Nonie. The love and determination were the same and maybe, in the end, that defined people the most: Did they love and did they fight, in one way or another, for what they believed in?

She was worried about Jael and Ash; I could see it on her face. She was happy I was safely back, but her kids—the ones she loved the most—were not. She was right to be worried, but I would do my best to protect her from that truth.

"Did you do okay?" she asked, placing a weathered hand against my face.

"Yes, Momma," I said, scooping her into a hug and feeling her bones against the loose skin.

Her age and her limp, which Jael told me she had always had, made it challenging for her to do much physical labor and so the muscles hadn't developed on her like they had on the rest of us. She had been plump before, and now she was thin, with skin that hung from her. She was not a pretty woman, and I loved her for it.

"They'll be back soon," I said, releasing her. "They're probably being cautious. There was a lot of gunfire. Not— not near them," I said as I registered the fear that came over her.

Haz came from behind me and placed a hand on Momma's back, and said, "What she meant was, they're being patient, waiting for the right opportunity."

"Detective," she said, "you and I have always had an honest relationship and by now you know my kids enough to realize there is no patience in them. They're beautiful children, but they aren't cautious or patient."

"They're soldiers," Haz said sternly. "They were trained to complete the mission, and the mission was to bring the woman they were rescuing back here safely. They might risk their own lives, but they won't risk hers."

Momma allowed her shoulders to release some of the tension they held. "Thank you. I needed to hear that."

"I've always told you the truth and this is no exception," he said.

"How long until you think they'll come home?" she asked.

"A day or two," Haz answered.

There was a time when a day or two with no communication was an eternity, but that was when my phone could tell me everything I wanted and connect me to anyone I wanted to be connected to in less than a minute. This life, as bizarre as it was, was so much more real than my old life. Then, I had a sense of being an actor in a movie, of the whole thing being made up. Those feelings were gone. Everything felt real.

"Hi, East," James said in delight as he loped toward me, arms wide open for a big bear hug.

Gus was completely wrong. I liked hugs. I squeezed James to me.

"How was your trip?" James asked, holding onto my hand.

"It was pretty good, James. How was everything here?"

"Good. Me, Dad, and Simon, and some of the other guys built our house. See? It's over there," he said proudly, pointing to a fairly large dwelling built in the spot that used to contain the lean-to Jonah and Bria had built.

"That's great," I said.

It seemed appropriate that James and his family would take the place that my brother had occupied. After all, it was because of Jonah and my friends that the Tait family had come here.

"John finally woke up," Haz said, spotting him stride toward us.

John was squinting in the bright light of the morning sun.

"Did he stay with you last night?" I asked, watching John stumble toward us.

Haz nodded. "I figured Ash wouldn't mind if John slept on his mat."

When John was about ten yards away his pace slowed and his face changed. He was staring at James. I blocked John's stare with my body.

Yes, James was different, but he was no less than the rest of us and he didn't deserve to be stared at. John adjusted his path, seeing past me as if I didn't exist. He came beside me, his hand moving toward James's face. James was startled, but didn't pull away.

"That's my son," Mr. Tait said, coming from behind Haz. There was protection in his voice, but not anger.

At the sound of Mr. Tait's voice, John's hand moved from James's face. He blinked as if remembering where he was. "Forgive me," he said, his voice breaking. "Forgive me."

The words were not meant for us. John turned, fleeing to the trees.

"Leave him," Haz said as I started after him.

"What if he takes off?" I said, startled by John's sudden shift in behavior.

"Then he does," Haz said. "He's not our prisoner. But I don't think he's going to leave. I think something about James triggered something in him."

"That happens when people see my kids," Mr. Tait said. "They remind people of something or someone. The young girl who was with your brother had a similar reaction to my son. She cried and cried."

James took my hand and said, "I held on to her tight so she wouldn't feel so sad."

"Yes, you did," Mr. Tait said. "You did a good thing. You helped her."

"Yes, I helped her. When that man comes back, I will hug him too. It will help him."

Mr. Tait was overcome with love for his son. "You're a kind boy, you know that?"

"Dad, you tell me that all the time," James said, rocking his body in bashful pride.

"It's the truth," Mr. Tait said, "and people should always tell the truth, especially if it's something good."

Mr. Tait placed a hand on the back of his son's neck, and the love they shared charged the space surrounding us.

Fifteen
BRIA

"I'm sorry, but I need to stop," Blaise said as she sunk to the ground.

Josh, Felicia, and Richard sat beside her.

Though Blaise was becoming stronger, it was still too much to ask her to walk more than a few miles at a time. The delay was painful. I understood how she must have felt when I was too weak to continue toward her parents and Sara's family. The desire to see my father and JP and all the others I loved was overwhelming. At this pace it would take at least two more days.

"Are you doing okay?" Sara asked me.

My impatience must have been noticeable. "Yes, just anxious to get home," I answered. "But it's okay. We'll be there soon." I said this more for my benefit than hers.

"It's funny," Sara said, "it's like no matter where we go, we're always leaving someone we love behind."

I wasn't sure that was funny as much as it was sad. I tried not to think of East and Haz and the others in our small town. I tried not to think of the danger they were in. I definitely did not allow myself to think of the sorrow Charlotte and Quint would experience when we told them their daughter was not with us. With those thoughts, I, too, dropped to the ground. I was no longer in a hurry. The sooner we returned, the sooner we would have to tell them. We wouldn't even have an instant of happiness. They would immediately notice who was missing, and ask. At least she wasn't dead. At least we didn't have to tell them that.

"I didn't mean to upset you," Sara said from beside me.

"Just thinking of East," I answered.

"I think of her so many times a day. I say a prayer for her every time she enters my mind."

I nodded, not so much in agreement than in a sort of acknowledgment of her words. There was nothing more to be said.

An hour later Blaise was on her feet and we were on our way. This was the first time we had walked this path. On the way north, we had been in the truck. We were east of the interstate and would eventually run right into my family's property. The vegetation was thick here, in the middle of summertime, and my feet were always sore and calloused. I longed for a pedicure. It was a senseless desire—such luxuries no longer existed.

It hadn't rained in days, which was good for walking, but it meant water was in short supply and we could only gather it from streams or ponds. And that made our path more of a zigzag than a straight line. We'd run out of purifying tablets, so we were back to filtering as best we could and then boiling. Between Blaise needing to rest and the added time to find water and purify it, the last twenty or forty miles were the longest and most agonizing. So many times, I wanted to start running to get closer to home, but every time I stopped myself. It wasn't wise. The others didn't want to run, Blaise couldn't, and running would cause the need for more water. Instead, I did what I could to help quicken the pace, while still allowing Blaise the rest she needed.

My left eye squinted as sunlight hit it. I turned. It was coming from the side.

"What is it?" Jonah asked as he followed my movement.

"The sun is being reflected by something," I said, instantly aware of what it was and wishing desperately I had not noticed.

Jonah stepped toward the reflection. "It's metal," he said with confusion.

He had not yet remembered, but he would.

Blaise stepped forward. "That must be the plane I saw," she said sadly.

Jonah stepped back.

"What plane?" Felicia asked.

There was silence.

"On the way up, it was the same," Blaise said. "The light reflected and we used the scope of a rifle to see what it was." She paused and briskly wiped the moisture from her eyes. "It was a plane. A passenger plane that crashed."

Juliette's face turned pale. "I don't want to see it," she whispered.

I pulled her long hair from her sticky back. "No, we won't go to it," I said, the memory of the crumpled train entering my mind. At least we hadn't actually seen the wreckage of the plane up close.

We turned, continuing in silence, until Juliette spoke.

"How did you come to be at the harvesters' camp?"

Her words surprised me—surprised all of us. We had not spoken of the harvesters' camp since we decided to allow Richard and Felicia to continue on with us. Their time there remained the elephant walking beside us that we pretended didn't exist.

Startled by Juliette's simple question, Felicia said, "Umm, the place we were when you found us?"

"Yes. How is it that you came to be there?" Juliette asked, the phrasing of her words reminding me of how little she belonged in this world of barren destruction.

"It's a long story," Felicia said.

"We have plenty of time," Juliette said graciously.

Felicia and Richard exchanged a glance. Felicia nodded at Richard, and he cleared his throat.

"After the snowstorm," Richard said, "we went to the animal shelter."

"We were worried the animals would freeze to death or starve," Felicia said. "We thought they would have a better chance of surviving in the wild than locked in cages."

Sage was walking beside Jonah and me. "Yeah, 'cause that makes sense," she mumbled so only we could hear. "Saving animals and shooting kids."

"On our way home we crossed paths with the sheriff," Richard said. "He was a friend of ours, and he asked if we could help him keep things under control."

"We agreed, of course," Felicia said enthusiastically. "And he put us in charge of our neighborhood."

Richard continued. "Once we got home, we did what we could to help those around us. But as the winter intensified, we realized that if we didn't do something, most of us weren't going to survive."

Felicia said, "That's when Jessica, the sheriff's wife, suggested we take all the food we had to the church and barbeque restaurant."

My head spun at the memory of that place, of the evil that it was.

"Almost everyone who was still alive went there. It was our only legitimate option—or at least, that's what we thought," Richard said. "Shortly after we got there, people started getting sick and shortly after that, a helicopter came and offered us food and medicine."

"In exchange for your weapons?" Josh asked.

"No, in exchange for crops," Richard said, a hint of something like remorse in his voice.

Felicia took his hand. "During the winter, we accumulated a bill that we agreed to pay once the ground thawed and we could plant crops."

"As you are aware," Richard added, "the winter was a difficult one."

"And every time the snow stopped, more people arrived, begging for food and heat and medicine. Our bill rose," Felicia explained. "But what could we do? We couldn't turn people away."

They still cared about people at this point, seeing them not as objects to control but as humans worthy of life. I wondered when that changed.

"In January," Richard said, "military trucks came, bringing the promised food and medicine, but they also carried soldiers and seeds."

"Once the ground thawed, we began to plant the seeds," Felicia said, "but what we owed them was so much more than we could produce and still eat our fill. We had to ration what people received. We had to, we had no choice. The workers began to get upset and some refused to work. It was easy for them. They weren't the ones dealing with DC. We were."

Richard squeezed his wife's hand and subtly shook his head, a signal to explain no more. "I believe we've answered your question, Juliette. That's how we came to be there and how things began. There is no more to be said."

*   *   *

"We can't allow them to stay with us," I pleaded quietly to the others when Blaise and Josh were away from us, sitting at the far end of camp with her parents.

Sara sat cross-legged, opposite me. "Bria, they explained things," she said.

"How can you say that?" I said, expecting Sara to be more upset by the killings than I was.

"People make mistakes. We should forgive them," Sara said sadly.

"Murder is not a mistake," Sage said. "Especially not how they did it. It was murder. No mistake, just murder."

"Would you have behaved differently?" Juliette said from beside Sara, her voice becoming stronger every time she spoke.

Sage and I stared at the girl. In turn, Sara gazed at us as if Juliette had somehow proved her point—a point I didn't understand.

"Are you asking if Sage would've shot those people?" I asked.

Juliette nodded. Sage and I exchanged a glance.

"Of course not," Sage said.

"Why not?" Juliette asked, tilting her head. The firelight illuminated half her face more than the other as twilight settled on our camp.

My words emerged slowly, in confusion: "Why would she kill them?"

Jonah lowered the stick he had been using to poke at the fire. "Bria, Juliette is not saying that the Sage today, with her experiences, would've walked into the camp and shot Annalise and her parents." His voice overflowed with sorrow at the girl's name. "But if she, or any of us, had Richard and Felicia's experiences, if we had been put in charge of the camp, if pressures increased from DC, if we lost sight of, or never internalized the objective truth that all life is sacred, then why not? Why wouldn't we kill, as they did?"

"Those are a lot of ifs," Sage said.

"Yes," Jonah replied, "but life is made up of ifs, of factors that change from one person to the other, of one time in history to the other."

"But they killed," Sage said.

"Yes, and Juliette's point is you would have, too. I would've, we probably all would've," Sara said, her voice thoughtful and patient.

"How can you say that?" Sage asked in anger. "How could you say I would've killed those people or that you would've? Mom raised us better than that!" Her voice broke at the mention of their mother.

148

"I'd like to think I wouldn't do what they did," Sara said to her sister, "and I want to believe it, but there's a part of me that understands that context matters, especially when you don't have objective truth to guide you."

Sage opened her mouth to object, but Sara continued. "You never met Blaise's parents before all of this. They were the two most wonderful, most genuine, most giving people. They were good to the very center of their being, and then this happened, and they … became murderers. I'm honest enough to recognize there is nothing so special about me that would prevent me from falling as badly—or even worse, if such a thing is possible."

"There but for the grace of God go I," Juliette said. "It's what my parents always told me when I became upset when people treated my brother poorly," she said, softly leaning into Sara.

"We aren't asking you to trust them," Jonah said. "I'm not prepared to do that yet and I don't think Blaise is either, but we're asking you to accept that good people can do bad things."

"Bad people can do good things, too," Sage said. "Maybe before, they were acting or pretending. Maybe at the camp, that was who they really are."

"They raised Blaise," I said. "They weren't pretending before. They committed one of the most heinous acts I could ever imagine and I will not trust them, but I will not stop them from moving forward with us." I was resigned to the fact that Sage and I were outnumbered, and accepting of the fact that the others were right. Richard and Felicia were not inherently evil people. I disagreed that Jonah, Sara, or Juliette in that situation would have murdered a child and her parents. That was completely wrong. But I did agree that to act differently, to not have treated those at the camp as objects to be controlled, would've taken an internal strength that most people, including me, didn't possess.

***

"You never would've killed those people," I whispered as I lay beside Jonah, listening to his heartbeat in the dark of night. A shooting star raced across the sky.

"Why do you think that?" he asked, rolling to his side. He rested his right hand on my hand that lay across my stomach.

"You don't care what the rest of the world says about you."

He moved his hand to my hair, pushing the short strands behind my right ear. "No, I guess I don't care much about that, but how would that have kept me from murdering those people?"

I rolled to my side to face him. "It's like you said. Richard and Felicia lost sight of the objective truth that all life has value. They also lost sight of the objective truth of who they were. They started seeing themselves in a certain way, a way the outside told them they should be, and they lost sight of who they actually were. It's like they stopped seeing themselves as good, and so they stopped being good. They started seeing themselves as commanders working for DC, who had to keep the slacker slaves in line, and so that's who they became."

"And they did whatever they needed to do to fulfill that image," Jonah said in agreement.

"Yes, but you aren't like that."

"I guess I'm not. I was when I was younger, but for a long time it hasn't been about how the world defines me."

"Why not?"

He lowered his head onto his arm and rolled onto his back, staring up at the stars. "I think I realized how easily the world's image of me changes. When I got arrested, no one from school wanted anything to do with me. Maybe they were right to make that choice, but they weren't right to see me differently. I wasn't different because I got arrested."

"You became bad," I said.

He smiled. "Yes, to them I became bad. A guy who beat up the poor state attorney's brother in a bar   that's what the media said about me. That's what people believed and so that's who I became to them. But I was no different. If anything, I was a better person, not worse, for my time in jail."

"Is that when you stopped caring what other people thought about you?"

"Bria, I'm no different than anyone else. I care what others think of me. Especially you. But there's a difference between caring what others think and letting that define how you think of yourself."

"That's what they did. Let it define them."

"Yeah, I think so," he said.

"It's weird. I always thought of them as so solid, like they had life figured out and they were doing it really well," I said, thinking back to when I had visited Blaise's house a few years ago.

"I'm sure they did, but when life changes so quickly, it's hard not to change with it."

"But you wouldn't," I said. "You didn't."

"You didn't either," he said, his fingers tracing the back of my hand.

I thought back to when the light exploded in the sky and how scared I was. "Only because you and East found us and your family allowed us to stay. If those things hadn't happened, I would've changed," I said, recognizing how scary that truth was. "But I don't think you would have."

He shrugged. "I try to be true to who God made me to be. It's easy to get caught up in a world that's on self-destruct, but recognizing that I'm made for more than this world helps me stay steady."

I lowered my head against his shoulder. His arm wrapped around my body, bringing me warmth in the chilly night air. He was asleep in minutes. My mind was drifting as I listened to his beating heart and the sounds of owls in the distance. The smell of honeysuckle mixed with the smell of dying embers. The peace of darkness brought an understanding of his words that I wouldn't have had if chaos surrounded us. This is how the world had been made. This was real. The drama of darkness that played out in our lives, that was not truly who we were. It was there to distract and derail us. It worked most times on most people, but not on Jonah. He understood who he was. He was able to see through the chaos and see the good, and by seeing the good he was able to be the good.

His hand fell from my hip to the ground. I rolled over, my back against his side, my head resting on his arm, my fingers looping through his fingers. In his sleep, he took my hand and held on tight.

I opened my eyes. Across the camp I saw Felicia and Richard sleeping beside one another. They went through life together, they made choices together. If one of them had gone against what the harvesters wanted from them, neither of them would have become a murderer. Near them, Sage sat, Astrea curled beside her. She leaned against a tree, one hand on her gun, the other on her stomach. She stared into the darkness.

My hand tightened around Jonah's. Never had I been so thankful for falling in love with a man who knew he was made for more.

Sixteen
BRIA

Jonah's hand was in mine. I squeezed it, not meaning to, but unable to stop. My body was tense. I needed to run—to get home. He squeezed back.

"I can't take this much longer," I whispered to him as Blaise rested beside the remnants of my ancestors' weathered fence. We were so close.

"You should go, Bria," Blaise said as she caught her breath. "I can tell this is painful for you. We only have a few miles left. Why don't you and Jonah go on ahead of the rest of us."

"I'm sorry," I said sheepishly. "Is it that obvious?"

Richard chuckled. "My dear, you look as if you are about to jump out of your skin, and who can blame you? Your father is there. You should go to him."

I felt guilty. It wasn't my father I longed to hug; it was JP.

Sara stood beside the fence, a hand resting on the faded post. "You and Jonah should go. We'll be there soon," she said.

"Is it safe for us to split up?" I asked.

Josh gestured to the fence. "We are literally in your backyard. What could happen?"

I raised an eyebrow.

Josh said, "Okay, a lot can happen. But it's unlikely."

"What do you think?" Jonah asked, squeezing my hand.

"We will have each other," I said, turning to him.

"And we will have each other," Blaise said, reassuring us.

"Wanna race?" I asked, unable to contain my excitement.

Jonah released my hand and started sprinting. I laughed, pushing hard to catch up. After a few minutes, he slowed his pace to match mine. We kept that pace for several miles.

"Wait, time out. I need to tie my boot," Jonah said, trying not to sound too out of breath.

"I'll slow down, but I'm not stopping," I said, continuing forward while he stooped to tie the laces.

I was getting closer and closer. The house was visible. I turned. Jonah was nowhere in sight. I decided not to wait. I was breathing heavily as I pushed my legs harder and harder. From the side, I saw movement and dove, instinctively pulling my gun as I rolled to my feet. A man moved from the trees that bordered the open yard. He had been watching the house. I pointed the gun, my heart racing.

I recognized him.

Heath. He had been with Mick. He was the one we had not killed. That was a mistake. A dog stood beside him, a dog whose head and shoulders were wide and terrifying, like Wrath's had been.

The dog saw me first. I moved my gun to the dog. It growled.

Heath's hands went into the air. The dog's hair stood on edge, just as Wrath's had done when it was about to attack JP.

"Why are you here?" I shouted, both hands on the handle of the pistol.

"I live here," Heath said, his voice shaking.

"Impossible," I shouted. I turned at the sound of footsteps. Jonah was behind me.

"I do," Heath said.

Jonah shouted to him, "Call off your dog."

"Franklin, sit," Heath commanded.

The dog whimpered and obeyed.

"Quinn, tell them."

I turned. She was there, raven hair shining in the midday sun, her eyes dark as charcoal, skin soft and pink like her mother's. I wanted to cry at the sight of her.

"Bria?" Her young voice spoke my name and I started to shake.

"Jonah?" She gasped as she ran toward us.

My eyes never left Heath's. He smiled as Quinn ran to us. Her arms wrapped tightly around me. My heart raced, my mind not understanding what was happening. Why was a murderer here? Was she a prisoner? Were the others dead?

"It's okay," she said, squeezing me as tight as she could. "He's not bad anymore."

Heath's arms fell to his side. "To be clear, I never actually was bad. Merely confused and misguided," Heath said in a joking tone.

"And my grandfather is dead as a result of it," Jonah screamed, his gun pointed.

Again, Heath's arms shot up.

"Jonah, we must forgive," Quinn said, releasing me and going to her brother.

"Where's Mom and Dad?" he asked, his voice tense and angry.

"In the house," Heath said. "They're all in the house. My wife and kids too. Please. I'm sorry. I didn't understand before. I've been with your family since April. Please, please ask them," Heath begged.

"Go!" Jonah said, signaling for Heath to begin walking toward the house.

Quinn went to walk beside the dog.

"No. Back here, Quinn," Jonah said, his gun aimed at Heath's back.

My gun was aimed at his head.

Quinn turned. "You're not the boss of me," she said. "Jesus is the boss of me, not you!"

Jonah blinked. His arms relaxed a little. If it were not for Heath, I would have laughed. She was so much like her mother.

"Go get Mom and Dad," Jonah said.

"Fine." She stormed off toward the house, the dog trotting after her.

Heath continued forward, his arms raised chest high.

As we neared the house, the door swung open and JP jumped from the steps. He sprinted to us. Ignoring the threat of our guns, he dove into my arms. I allowed my gun to fall as his hug tackled me to the ground.

"You're alive!" he shouted as tears started to spill from my eyes.

I couldn't speak. I held him and kissed his blonde hair.

"What about me?" Jonah said as he continued to point his gun at Heath.

"You're alive too!" JP said, helping me up and wrapping his arms around his brother.

Jonah stooped to hug him with one arm, pulling him into a tight embrace. I picked up my gun and pointed it at Heath.

Behind Heath, the others came streaming out of the house. Charlotte, Quint, my father, and Eli, who was helping Nonie. Behind them came a woman with dark skin and dark wavy hair and two young children. A boy and a girl.

"Put the guns down," Quint said as he ran toward us.

I slipped the gun against my hip. Jonah put his away. Heath had been telling the truth. He was not a threat, at least not at this moment.

My father held my face between his hands and sobbed. They were rough and calloused. The lines on his face were deeper than when I'd left. The outsides of the lines were sunburned, the insides white.

"You came back to me," he cried.

"I promised I would," I said, wrapping my arms around him. Though I couldn't see her, I sensed my mom was there too.

When my dad finally released me, Nonie was there to scoop me up ... her hands soft against my sun-cracked skin, her embrace gentle and loving. I was so thankful for her love. After her, Eli pulled me tight, saying he was thankful I was alive.

"Something's different about you," Eli said, his eyes staring deep into mine and his hands touching my short hair.

"A lot is different," I said, not wanting to discuss any of it, enjoying the overwhelming love.

Charlotte came after Eli, and as she released me. "The others?" she said, her voice catching in her throat.

As I had imagined, she was grateful for us, but longed for her daughter.

As if on cue, the rest of our group appeared from the woods. Immediately the hugs began again. I was grateful for the joy before the sorrow came. Astrea ran to Quinn, who giggled when the dog licked her face. In that way, she was nothing like her mother. JP introduced himself to Juliette, who stood silently beside Sara. She was not hiding and she was not cowering. Instead, she shook his hand and whispered her name. She introduced Astrea and the three of them took turns petting her.

Blaise introduced her parents to the others. I cringed when my father shook Richard's hand. I did not believe they would kill anyone I loved. If I did, I never would have allowed them here. But I did not believe they would add goodness, either.

Charlotte came to us, Quint by her side, with a hand over her shoulder. Jonah held my hand.

She leaned her head against her son's chest, unable to look him in the eye. "Is your sister ...?" Her voice caught.

"She's not dead, Mom."

Charlotte burst into tears, her arms wrapping around his waist. He released my hand and held her as she cried. Quint had a hand on each of them as he stared into Jonah's eyes.

"She chose to stay," Jonah said.

"Stay?" Quint asked.

"There's a war, Dad," Jonah said, his voice taking on a degree of intensity that conveyed more than his words. "It's for our country, and she chose to stay and fight."

Charlotte sobbed and released Jonah, clinging to Quint as if her life depended on it. We watched him hold her. Both of them cried for their daughter who was willing to fight—not from a place of hatred but from a place of love. For their daughter, who was the bravest person any of us had ever known.

Seventeen
BRIA

I was overcome by the sense of belonging and home as I entered my great-grandparents' home. The smell of food and burning wood. The luxury of safety and of pure running water that came deep from under the earth. Long ago I never would have described such things as luxuries, but now I did. I understood it's possible to survive without them. I had done it for almost four months.

As soon as I entered the kitchen, fatigue washed over me. The reality of all we had been through weighing me down, I collapsed on the hearth at the side of the wall-sized oven. Jonah sat beside me, and JP squeezed in between us.

My friends sat around the kitchen table.

"I didn't realize how exhausted my body was," Sara said, laying her head on her arm that was sprawled across the table.

My father and Eli handed out glasses of water. The smooth glass felt unnatural against my cracked lips and calloused palms. I held the cold, clear water in my mouth, enjoying its coolness before allowing it to enter my body.

Richard and Felicia sat at the other side of the oven, on stones purposefully placed to create seating. My great-grandparents had thought of everything. We were all here, all except Heath and his family.

I had accepted that they were not an immediate threat. I doubted they would hurt us, but I was pleased when they didn't follow us into the house.

Sage sat beside Sara. From where I sat and where she sat, I could see Sage's belly was larger than it had been; her face, too, was fuller. Before the light, that small amount of weight gain would have been imperceptible, and still was to most people. Sage needed to tell the others soon, before they guessed on their own.

My father finished handing out glasses and came and sat beside me.

"What happened to your head?" he asked, his fingers reaching toward my scalp.

"It's a long story," I said, evasively moving my head from his touch.

"Trent," Sara said.

"Trent?" My father blinked in confusion and then understanding. "He ... he did that to you?"

"It's okay, Dad. I survived and the headaches have stopped." I took my dad's hand in mine.

There would be time to go into the details of the last few months, but this was not that time. I was here, I was alive. My skull had healed and my brain seemed to have, too. But there was another who was not here. Who may or may not be alive. My story didn't matter.

Hers did.

"Where did she stay?" Charlotte finally asked, her voice cracking with tears.

Jonah finished his water. I wanted to take his hand, to offer him my strength, but JP sat between us. I didn't want him to have to answer this alone, but he was their son and she was their daughter. In the end it was about their family, not me or my friends.

Jonah rubbed the smooth glass. "There's a town, a peaceful town north of DC. We stayed there after we fled the city. There are other people living there that we trust. Good people that are willing to fight for what's right."

"They promised not to attack DC yet," I said, hoping that might lessen the worry Charlotte and Quint must be feeling.

"Attack DC?" Charlotte said.

I bit my lip. I shouldn't have said that. They weren't aware that was even a possibility.

"Things are different, Mom," Jonah said. "The government has changed—or at least the parts we saw. People are fighting for power and those that have it are fighting for more. The truths that built this country have been lost. It's being rebuilt with lies. East couldn't allow that to happen."

"She's taking on the government?" Eli said in fear.

"She and others are figuring out what to do. Their first step was to go to Camp David. Haz, the man who helped us escape DC, said some prisoners there may be able to help. East and the others were going there to learn what they could," Jonah said, rotating the glass in his hands.

"Camp David?" Eli asked with the same worry and fear. "How is that better than DC?"

Eli didn't understand; he hadn't seen what we'd seen or experienced what we'd experienced.

"It's better," my dad said, his jaw clenched as he spoke.

He had seen and experienced, and done so before there was any sense of order. I shuddered at the thought. He squeezed my hand tighter. We understood what the other had lived through.

Quinn crawled onto Jonah's lap. "Why didn't you make her come home?" she asked him with tears filling her eyes.

My shoulders slumped. I hadn't thought of that: Jonah would be blamed and held responsible for his sister. The others wouldn't say it, but they must all be thinking it. Why didn't you fight for her? Why didn't you drag her home? Why did you abandon her?

He gave Quinn a quick hug and said, "She stayed because she loves us so much." He rested his face on her hair.

"No!" Quinn shouted, pushing away from Jonah's supporting arms. "She doesn't love us. She didn't even come home."

Jonah's heart was breaking ... I could feel it.

Quint released his wife, who was crying, and went to Quinn. He scooped her up from his son, and said, "Quinn, East loves you more than you will ever understand, and she is braver than anyone else in this world. She never would've stayed for any reason other than love."

"Not coming home is not love!" Quinn shouted angrily at her father.

She was four, and her understanding of love was kindness. To her, East's actions were not kind.

Charlotte held out her hands. Quinn went to her and snuggled against her neck. Quint put his arms around both of them as their bodies shook with tears.

After several minutes, Nonie handed her handkerchief to Charlotte, who wiped her eyes and Quinn's nose.

Charlotte sniffed as she stared down into Quinn's eyes. "Honey," she said, "East has always made sacrifices for those she loves. You can't remember, but when you were born she made the very biggest sacrifice for you because she loves you the very most ..." Charlotte's voice cracked.

Quint's arms tightened around them.

The note East had given me felt heavy in my pocket.

"That's how love works," Quint said. "You can't remove sacrifice from love. It's impossible. That's confusing, but it's the truth, and East understands that truth better than anyone."

"It's the reason she stayed," Jonah said softly. "She loves us too much to not fight for us." His voice sounded sad.

Quinn wiggled free from her parents and came back to Jonah. She placed her hands on his beard. "She shouldn't love us so much."

Jonah couldn't hold back any longer. His shoulders rocked as his tears fell. He had been so strong for so long. He loved his sister and he had let her stay behind. How much that must have hurt him—how much, I didn't understand when we had left the town.

"Quinn, it's how she was made," JP said, one small hand on Jonah's shoulder, the other on his little sister's back. "She was made like Mom. They love us, even when they're mean to us and tell us what to do all the time. That's their way of showing us love, and East loves us."

"Well, I don't love her!" Quinn stomped her feet as she started to cry. "I don't! I don't love her at all. I hate her! She left me and I hate her!"

Charlotte sobbed into Quint's chest.

My heart broke, watching Jonah's blood-red eyes beg Quinn to understand.

Juliette stood and went to Quinn. "Quinn, when we left your sister, she told me how much she loves you and John Paul. She spoke of how wonderful you both are and she asked me if I would do something for her. Do you know what that something is?"

"Tell us that she loves us," Quinn said, her arms crossed in anger.

"Yes," Juliette said, "but she also asked me to fill in for her."

"Fill in for her?" Quinn said.

"She didn't want to leave you, even for a short time, without a big sister, so she asked me if I would be your big sister until she got home. But the trouble is, I have never been a big sister. I was the little sister in my house." Her voice caught. She blinked and continued. "I told this to East and she said all I needed to do was ask you and you would help me. She said you were the best little sister and thanks to you, she had become the best big sister, and I would too."

Quinn's arms unfolded.

"Would you help me?" Juliette asked. "Would you help me learn how to be a big sister?"

Quinn nodded and began to cry as she went to her parents. Her mother lifted her and both her parents held her.

"I don't hate her," Quinn said, sobbing. "I love her and I want her home."

"We all do, baby," Charlotte said, their tears combining. "We all do."

Eighteen
BRIA

Holding my hand, JP guided me into the yard. Jonah followed us, with Eli beside him. The two walked in silence, though so much needed to be said.

"The barn looks good," I said as we neared the stone structure with new fences and a solid roof.

JP beamed. "Me and Heath have been working on it. Dad and Eli sometimes too, but mostly me and Heath."

I put my arm around his shoulder. "You've gotten taller too," I said.

"I have," he said proudly.

"Why'd you build it like that?" Jonah asked from behind us.

As we neared, I understood his question. A fence had been built around the entrance to the barn—that part made sense—but what was strange were the multiple low branches that had been placed against the fence, blocking off anything from getting in or out at the ground level. Though, no predator would be deterred by it.

"You'll see," JP said excitedly.

The ground inside the fence was dirt and mud; not even a single blade of grass remained. Once we reached the edge of the fence I could see that in one corner there lay two good-sized hogs.

"They're hogs, not pigs," JP said, "but they're still meat and there is lots you can do with their fat, and if you cook up their skin it's kind of crunchy, like potato chips used to be."

I grimaced at how disgusting everything he had said was. "I did not realize that."

"It's not as gross as you think," Eli said, joining us at the fence.

"It's not gross at all. It's the circle of life," JP asserted.

Jonah studied the fence until he found the gate. He went to it and walked through the dirt, into the barn. I followed, practically running.

Talin was there in a stall with Fulton. She threw up her head and whinnied, excited to see me. I wrapped my arms around her and rubbed my face against her neck. She leaned into my embrace as if returning the hug. It felt so good to hold her.

Beside us, Jonah was petting Fulton, their eyes locked as if communicating in a language only they understood.

"It's good to be home," he said.

"So good," I said.

"What was it like?" JP asked, in a tone that reminded me of the hyper child I had met on Thanksgiving.

I turned from Talin to face him. His eyes were alive with curiosity. Never. I never wanted him to know what it was like in the rest of the world. I never wanted him to lose the innocence that he held on to.

"It was different," I said.

"We're happy to be home," Jonah added.

"But East isn't," JP said with questioning sadness.

"It's too early to discuss all of that," Eli said, his hand on his brother's shoulder. "Besides, something tells me they have something more exciting to announce." He winked at JP.

I stared in amazement. "How did you know?"

"What?" JP said.

Jonah was watching the exchange with amused exhaustion, his arm around Fulton.

"I'm a priest. God tells me everything," Eli said, teasing. "Plus, I overheard Sara and Blaise talking as they went up the stairs, about needing to make sure your mom's wedding dress fit you."

"Wedding dress?" JP made a weird face.

"Bria and I are engaged," Jonah said, beaming with pride.

"That's not so exciting," JP said.

Eli said, "She's going to be our sister. How is that not exciting?"

"She already was my God sister and I already think of her as a sister. I mean, it's exciting for Jonah—he gets to marry her—but it's not so exciting for the rest of us," JP said, his hands in his pockets as he kicked at the ground.

"Did *you* want to marry her?" Jonah asked, twisting his body to gently nudge his brother.

"No!" JP said a little too loudly.

Jonah and Eli smirked at each other.

"I was sort of hoping that you could officially be my little brother," I said, putting my hands on his shoulders. "I've never had one and I've always wanted one. Sometimes wives get angry at their husbands, but I'm pretty sure big sisters never get angry at little brothers."

"East always did," he said, his arms crossed.

"Oh … that's different," I assured him.

Putting an arm around me, Jonah said, "What if we let you be in the wedding?"

"Oh, fine," JP said, "but I still don't think it's exciting. Happy, I guess, but not exciting."

I leaned against Jonah, my body threatening to collapse, I was so tired. It was something about being home and safe. I could barely fight the sleepiness.

"All right, that's enough talking. You two need to bathe and you need to sleep," Eli said, turning to leave the barn. "The others should be done getting cleaned up. It wouldn't surprise me if Sage was already asleep. She appeared particularly tired." He gave me a knowing glance.

How was he so perceptive?

"But …" JP began.

"Eli's right. Look at us," Jonah said, gesturing, and I saw us with different eyes. We were filthy, our clothes torn, his hair and beard long and unkempt, our shoes caked with mud. I was sure we must smell, but it had been so long since I was clean that I wasn't able to smell us.

Inside, Richard and Felicia were bathing. The rest of our group was in various stages of falling asleep in the family room and living room. Heath and his family had taken over the girls' room upstairs, and Nonie and Quinn had turned the living room into their room. When I asked about them losing their room, Nonie said it had been her idea, that the stairs had been too difficult for her and the living room was better and larger. Sara, Sage, and I would join them there.

Jonah would go with his brothers and my father into the boys' room. Josh and Blaise returned to the nursery room. Richard and Felicia would sleep in the family room. As much as Eli liked to say "The more the merrier," we now counted nineteen people. More was no longer merrier. We needed more space, at least during the summer when we did not fear freezing or starving to death. During the winter it might make sense to have so many of us in one space. It was safer and warmer. But in the summer it was stifling.

"It's your turn," JP said, as I sat drifting off at the kitchen table.

I had insisted that Jonah take the next bath. I wanted to go last. I wanted to not feel rushed.

My hands slid up the banister as I climbed the stairs, my bare feet against the stone steps. I had slipped off my shoes, leaving them outside. The socks were rags that even Nonie doubted could be used for much more than cleaning. The upstairs was quiet. Those who were up there were asleep or falling asleep. Sleep was all I could think of, but I was too dirty even to lie on the floor.

The air in the bathroom felt warm, the tub inviting, with clean water and hot river rocks lining the bottom of the painted metal. I slipped my clothes off, the floor already dirty from the clothes my friends had shed before me. I fought the urge to look in the mirror. What would I see? A woman with a mud-stained, sunburned face framed by short, tangled hair.

I went instead to the water, my feet surrendering to the warmth, the rest of my body following as I slid the rocks to one end, making room for me. The soap was still wet from Jonah's use. It was infused with rosemary. Before we left, Nonie had said she was going to experiment with herbs in the soap. Charlotte said only if there was more than enough to eat. The rosemary plants must've been growing well.

As the soap slipped over my body, turning brown from the dirt, I felt Nonie's love. In everything she did, there was love. I placed the soap on the slats of wood used to hold it and leaned my back against the cool metal. My eyes closed, and I slipped my head under the water. Warmth and peace enveloped me. The world no longer mattered. In the water there was silence; in the water there was solitude. Perhaps that's why I had always liked swimming so much. In water, even back then, I felt some sense of peace.

I lifted my head and opened my eyes. So much inside of me had changed. So much outside of me had changed. The crazy thing was I had accepted it. I had become a warrior, though it was not my nature. But I had become what I needed to be to survive. As before, I had become someone who hid from silence. Neither of these people was really me; they were who I became when I had to. My true nature was this: calm, peaceful. Filled with silence. I had hidden from that nature for so long—my whole life. After the light, I was forced to realize it and, once I did, I was forced to put it aside as I became a warrior. Now, finally, I could be me, the person I had been created to be.

I sat forward and pulled the plug, watching the water swirl away. I was home.

Nineteen
EAST

It had been six days since my group made it back. Two days later, Jael and Ash showed up, with Pam hobbling beside them. She wasn't used to walking so far. Her feet were covered in blisters, like Sara's had been when we left our house for Bria's house. It was four days later and Pam was still hobbling around, though no longer covered in rags and dirt.

Members of the town had donated clothes to both John and Pam and they had bathed. John had combed the mats from his hair. It was pulled back, tied with a strip of leather, into a ponytail. His beard had been trimmed as evenly as he could, using scissors. Pam's hair was long and braided. The whiteness of it told me it had once been blonde like mine. They were not part of our conversation, but they were close enough to listen if they wanted to. It was clear from their postures that they wanted to.

Becca and Momma Pryce were standing with us as we stared at maps. They would not fight or leave the safety of the town, but they had good instincts and we were grateful for their thoughts.

"It's been four days," Jael said from her spot beside Momma Pryce. "They're not coming back."

179

I was thinking the same thing, and had been for two days, but didn't want to be the one to say it.

Becca said, "They could be on their way."

She was always so optimistic. She reminded me of Blaise, in that way. Though Blaise was a bit more realistic—the perfect blend of seeing things for how they were, while still holding on to hope. Becca, I was told, was more like Sara's late mother, Faith: unwilling to see the negative.

I leaned forward. "There was a lot of gunfire that first night," I said, offering the possibility of Seth and Derrick still being alive.

"And the next day and night," Ash added.

Jael said, "Should we search for them?"

I felt my insides twist. I didn't want to search for either of them. Seth, I didn't like, and Derrick, I hated. It wasn't right to hate, but it wasn't right to destroy the world, either.

"At this point they're either badly wounded, dead, or captured," Haz said. "We'll need to be prepared for any of those three scenarios."

"Meaning what?" John asked, stepping from the log and coming toward us.

"Meaning, be prepared to carry out the wounded, or the dead," Haz said.

Jael snapped the twig she had been rolling between her fingers. "Or figure out how to actually break into Camp

David, since I doubt they'd be stupid enough to let them wander around the yard again," she said.

John turned back to Pam. She didn't stand, but she shook her head.

"What is it?" I asked.

"Tell them," John said, turning to Pam, his back to us.

"Tell us what?" Haz said, stepping toward Pam and John.

"Don't search for them," Pam said.

Haz took another step toward them, arms crossed. "Why's that?"

They'd held back information. This was clear and it was not acceptable.

"You remember Derrick helped create all of this?" John said, his hand waving in the air as if Derrick had created the sky.

"We haven't forgotten," Haz said in anger.

Pam exchanged a glance with John. He nodded.

"He said he still had connections," Pam said. "And our existence is proof that someone believed him. He is the only reason they let us live."

I took a step toward them. "What does that mean, connections?" I asked.

"He said he could fix this if he got to Raven Rock," John said. "He said if he could speak with people there, he could fix things, change them to how they were supposed to be."

"Raven Rock?" I asked.

Haz said to me, "It's one of the government's underground bunkers."

"It's more than an underground bunker," Pam said. "It's the key to the continuity of government, to ensuring the United States survives."

"It's the place where high-ranking officials go to save themselves while the rest of us die," Ash retorted.

"No, not Raven Rock," Pam said. "Raven Rock is about the government surviving, not the people in the government. It's about keeping the Constitution and democracy intact."

"How do those things stay alive without the people?" Momma Pryce asked, her tone skeptical.

Pam replied, "Oh, people are kept alive too, but not necessarily the ones you'd think. People like the president and cabinet members are expendable. They can be replaced, and at Raven Rock they are replaced, in a fairly convoluted line of succession. This is done to keep the country functioning at the highest level possible."

"We've seen what the government is doing," Ash said, "and they aren't fixing things, that's for sure."

He was right. They were the problem, not the solution.

John stepped forward and said, "We've been thinking about that. You said those in charge have been in charge since almost right after the EMPs, correct?"

"Yes," Haz said with an edge of curiosity to his voice.

John nodded. "They were probably some of the same ones who took us to Camp David." He was speaking to Pam. Their expressions turned thoughtful, as if trying to figure something out.

Ash asked, "What does that matter?"

Pam stood, wincing as she did so. "Derrick was adamant that they had no right to hold us there and … no right to kill those that they did."

"What does that matter?" Jael asked.

"We aren't sure," Pam said, "but Derrick was adamant about getting to Raven Rock. He believed things would be better if he were there."

"You aren't sure, but you have a guess," Momma Pryce said. "What is it?"

Pam nodded to John, an apparent signal that it was okay to share their secret.

John put his hands in his back pockets. It was a position of great vulnerability, a position I avoided. "We think that those who are currently in charge are rogue," he said.

"Rogue?" I said.

"The government is slow," John said. "It's always been slow. It wouldn't have been organized only a few days after the attack, to do much of anything   let alone lock down DC and take all the politicians prisoner."

"And more than that, it wouldn't want to," Pam said, fighting back tears with anger. "What difference did we make to it? Why couldn't we have stayed with our families?"

"We were seen as a threat," John said. "But not by the US government. They couldn't have cared less."

"Then, by who?" I asked.

John shrugged. "Our guess is whoever wanted to take power."

Ash said, "You think those in control of the government aren't really part of the government?"

"We think those in charge of *DC* aren't part of the government," John clarified. "The point of the continuity of government was to continue the government and therefore the country as it was, not change it. You said laws are being rewritten, and while martial law certainly would have been instituted, the actual laws wouldn't have changed. That's the whole reason for places like Raven Rock existing, to keep that from happening."

Silence enveloped the space between us as we thought about their theory. Those in charge were only in charge because others followed their orders. They had no power. No real military force. We'd seen a few helicopters and lots of weapons, but was that the extent of their military power?

"The reason the navy and the air force are staying away?" Haz said, wonder in his voice.

"Have they stayed away?" Pam asked.

Haz nodded. "The guy in charge of most of DC—they call him the commander—spread the information that the troops couldn't be controlled, they'd desert if they came ashore, and they were needed to protect our borders."

"There is probably truth to that," John said. "They would be charged with keeping up our borders. But if we are correct, he would never have the authority to summon them back to the mainland—or have them do anything, for that matter."

"Where is it?" I asked. "Where is Raven Rock?" I wanted to go there to find what could be found and end this siege.

"Not far," Jael said. "If Derrick and Seth went there, they would've gotten there about the same time we got here."

"So that means they would've been there for three or four days," I said, louder than I meant to.

Haz said, "It also means we could be there in a day."

"We should take them with us," Ash said, referring to John and Pam. "They at least know that Derrick guy. I bet they'll recognize other people too."

John shifted; he was uneasy.

"What is it?" Momma Pryce asked him.

He looked around at the group. "I understand why you want to go there," he said, "but I hope you understand that I can't. I've been here longer than I wanted to be, and it's time for me to be going on."

John was trying to sound tough, as if we couldn't stop him—which of course we could—but we wouldn't. He wasn't our prisoner.

"I see," Momma Pryce said. "And where is it that you are going?" Her voice sounded amused, like she was talking to a child.

"To find my wife and kids," John said defensively.

I lowered my head. Did he not understand they were almost certainly dead?

"DC is not the same place you left eight months ago," Haz said, his jaw flinching as he remembered his city.

"I have to try," John said.

"You won't find them, but I respect you for trying," Jael said.

Sometimes she was too blunt. This was one of those times.

"Jael, that was too much," Momma Pryce rebuked. "How could he not try to find them? Of course he must go to DC and search for those he loves. Would you have done any differently if I had still been there?"

Jael shook her head.

"That's what I thought," Momma Pryce said. "It would seem to me that you all are splitting up."

"Momma?" Jael said, confused.

"He can't go by himself. He'll never make it. No offense, son," she said to John.

"None taken, but they've already risked their lives enough for me. Besides, my life doesn't matter anymore," John said matter-of-factly.

I understood his thinking. To him, his life existed for his family and without them his life made no difference. This, to him, was as true as any truth could be.

"All lives matter," Momma Pryce countered. "And they've been wanting to go to DC. Now they have a reason to also go to Raven Rock."

It's true we had considered going first to Camp David and then to DC, but no timeline had been established. It was also true that, given the new information, we needed to go to Raven Rock.

"What about this place?" Ash asked, speaking about the town. "Without us, there aren't a lot of people who can fight, leaving it and all of you vulnerable."

"If you all do your jobs correctly, there will be no need for us to fight," Momma Pryce said, winking at Ash, her eyes small and watery. "Besides, you four want to change the world and you aren't going to do that here."

"What about you?" Jael asked with concern and sadness. She loved Momma, and it was easy to understand why.

"Honey, you were never called to serve me," Momma Pryce said, her hand patting Jael's face. "I was called to serve you and it was one of the greatest honors of my life. But you're grown. You're a soldier and your country needs you. It needs all of you."

Jael took Momma's hand in her own and kissed it. "You're the best mother anyone could ever have," she said, pulling Momma's fragile frame in for a hug.

"And don't you forget it," Momma said lightheartedly, as she took Jael into her arms.

"I want to go to Raven Rock and find Derrick," Pam said, once Momma Pryce released Jael.

Ash said, "What will you do when you find him?"

"I will talk to him, something I should've done more of before all of this," Pam said.

"You will talk?" Ash's tone was sarcastic.

"Don't underestimate him," Pam said. "I did, and it was a mistake—a deadly one. I won't do that again. He believed he could change things if he was there. I want to go there and learn what he's planning. Besides, I have no reason to return to DC. It holds only pain for me."

"DC is my city," Haz said. "I owe it to her to be there."

"That means East will also be going to DC," Ash said with a smirk.

My face burned.

"If it's up to me, she will," Haz said, his voice strong and deliberate.

"Right, then. Jael and me will be going with Pam and the two lovebirds will be with John," Ash joked.

"Watch it," Haz said.

Ash chuckled.

"Cut it out, Ash," Jael said.

She and I had talked. We agreed Haz and I would be good together, but not long-term. We had too many differences, inside and out, to truly understand where the other was coming from. We weren't like Bria and my brother, who had grown up together and shared family. Haz and I had nothing in common. The only thing we shared was the desire to protect and defend those who needed it, and that wouldn't make a marriage. Especially not a marriage rooted in shared faith, like my parents and grandparents had. Jael said if I ever wanted to stop him cold, to tell him I didn't believe in sex before marriage. She said that would scare off any guy. I thought Haz might be an exception, but when I told her that, she laughed. She was probably right.

"Yeah, I'm with Haz," I said in a tone that dared Ash to make a comment.

He chuckled to himself and walked away.

Twenty
BRIA

"Do you think my mom is happy?" I asked as Eli and I sat beside the graves of my mother and brother.

"Happy? About you and Jonah?"

I nodded.

He leaned back, his legs outstretched, elbows bent, supporting his back. He appeared as if he was relaxing on a country picnic, not in an ancient family cemetery. In some ways his comfort with the setting made me uneasy; in other ways it made me believe him when he spoke of the communion of saints and how little death does to separate us from those holy souls we love, as he often referred to my mother and brother and Pops.

"Yes," Eli said, "I think she is."

"Because Jonah's really cute?" I asked, teasing. I needed him to say more than "Yes, I think she is."

"Your mom was a perceptive woman. I'm sure my brother's cuteness is not lost on her," he said in a lighthearted way, "but he is good, and he loves you, and he's Catholic. To someone like your mom who was, or is,"—he looked puzzled—"so devout, Jonah sharing that same faith would have, or does mean the world to her."

Even for a priest, the communion of saints must be a little confusing.

"What about your parents?" I said, suddenly realizing that while they had seemed excited that I was about to become their daughter-in-law, they might not be. Not really. If it was important to my mom that the man I married be Catholic, it was likely important to Quint and Charlotte that the person Jonah married was too.

Eli gazed at me quizzically. "You know they love you. So why would you ask that question?"

"I'm not Catholic and I'm not good ... but I do love him."

"First of all, you are good. Second, they love you like a daughter, and third, you agreed to allow Jonah to raise any kids you might have in the Church. It would be ideal if you two shared the same faith, but it is far from necessary. If I had to guess, I would say that my parents are hoping you eventually join the faith. But that's between you and God, and they will not interfere."

"My dad is hoping the same thing and he's not afraid to interfere," I said, not bothering to hide my irritation.

I'd been home for less than two weeks and every chance he got he tried to talk to me about God's unending mercy and the beauty and richness of the Church. It sounded nice at first, but it quickly became obnoxious.

Eli sat up. "Your dad feels tremendous guilt over his having taken the faith from you as a child."

"If I get there, it will be on my own time, not his," I said, frustrated with my dad.

"I understand that and Jonah does too. So does your dad. He's just impatient."

"And filled with guilt," I said.

"And filled with guilt."

"Coming to believe in God and then Jesus was one thing, but believing in all the stuff Catholics believe in is like a whole twenty other things," I said, trying to explain myself even though Eli had never asked for an explanation.

"It's not for the uncommitted, that's for sure." Eli teased. "And I understand that, Bria. I think it's awesome you believe in the existence of both God the Son and the Father. If you someday have a relationship with them and the Church, that's great, and if you don't, you don't. If you were a militant atheist as your dad had raised you to be, I think you and Jonah making a marriage work would be almost impossible. But if you can believe that marriage is a covenant between the two of you and God, that you are fully giving yourself to Jonah and Jonah is fully giving himself to you ... and that you are in it for life, and you will be open to life ... then, you are starting out better than a lot of marriages—including those between two Catholics who don't understand or accept those things."

I did agree with those aspects of marriage. Sara and Eli had expanded on Jonah's scripted explanation of marriage being a covenant, and it actually was rational. Well, rational if you believed in God, which still seemed a bit irrational. However, I had somehow become sure of his existence. Nonie had explained this to me. She said faith was about going beyond the rational—beyond what could be physically observed. I understood how people might struggle with this, but to me it made perfect sense. There was more to me than could be physically observed. Even if my brain was hooked up to monitors, it would not explain how my thoughts came to be, and I supposed the world was the same way. Science provided a basic understanding of why things were the way they were, but it could not explain the depths of it. Marriage, when done well, had always struck me as something that science struggled to explain. Sex was easily explained, but marriages where spouses selflessly give to one another in complete fidelity, that made no sense.

Eli leaned forward. "I think you're right, Bria, my parents aren't happy. They're overjoyed. You are literally the answer to a lifetime of prayers."

"A lifetime of prayers?" It was hard to imagine I was the answer to even one prayer, let alone a lifetime's worth.

"Yes, they've prayed for our spouses since we were babies. You are the answer to that prayer. Besides, you're also really cute and, at the end of the day, it's all about how cute the grandkids will be," he said with a teasing wink.

I laughed. "Nonie has already started hinting about grandkids—or, I guess, for her, great-grandkids."

"Give it a few months of being married," Eli said, "and she will be doing more than hinting."

"I feel way too young to be a mom," I said, hoping he'd spread the information that there were no babies planned anytime soon—thanks to the somewhat gross knowledge Charlotte had shared with Blaise and me about using fertility awareness to naturally space children.

Eli said, "And you should respect that feeling. If you two aren't ready, you aren't ready. Besides, once Sage's baby arrives, Nonie will have her baby fix and leave you and Blaise alone."

"Yeah, that will be helpful," I said, remembering when Sage had told everyone she was pregnant.

There had been silence. Complete silence as people swallowed the food in their mouth. JP was the first to speak, his question so innocent had brought forth a flood of tears. "She's married?" he'd blurted out.

Sara ran after Sage, catching up with her on the other side of the barn. The two were gone a long time. Charlotte and Maria had put their children to bed before they returned, Sara holding Sage's hand and beaming with love for her.

That's when I knew, really knew, everything was going to be okay.

"What was the father like?" Eli asked, sitting cross-legged, back straight, face thoughtful.

"Not cute, that's for sure," I said, shaking my head.

"So, any cuteness in that baby will be from Sage. Got it," Eli said, making light of the painful situation.

"Sage has always dated guys that are beneath her, both in looks and brains. Hopefully, for the baby's sake, Hayden was better than the rest. If he is, I didn't see it."

"Leaving her while she's pregnant with his child is not a good indicator of quality," Eli said.

"No, definitely not," I said. My heart ached for her.

"She doesn't appreciate her own worth," Eli said sadly. "So many women don't, and men too, for that matter. It's a shame they sell out for so little."

"You remember you're speaking to the biggest sellout of them all, before I met Jonah," I said.

"I realize that, but you do too. And if you know the truth and you accept the truth, it won't offend you."

He was right. His words hadn't offended me. I hated that I had made the choices I made, and it was difficult to accept that Sage had done the same thing—sold out for so little—but it was the truth.

"I think, for Sage it was the loss of her mom. She wanted to run from it," I said.

"And she did, by running to Hayden," Eli said.

I nodded. "It's sad that she'll be paying for that choice for the rest of her life."

"A baby is not a punishment, Bria, it's a gift," Eli said softly. "Sage has been given a tremendous gift."

"I doubt she'll be thinking that while she's in labor," I said. It was easy enough for him to say a child was a gift; he would never be the one pushing it from his body.

"No," he said, shaking his head. "Not during the worst of the pain, but after. When her child snuggles against her, when her ability to love grows exponentially, she will see what a gift her baby is."

"Why do men tell you they love you and then leave?" I asked, my head lying against my knees that were pulled up to my chest.

"Talk is cheap," he said curtly.

"That's a cliché," I mumbled.

"It may be, but it's true. It's the reason weddings are done in public, so everyone can testify to the promises made."

"I never knew that."

"Think about all the promises you've heard in the dark of night."

My face flushed with embarrassment at the memories of the men before Jonah.

"How many of those were truthful? How many of those men did as they promised?"

I lowered my head. He knew the answer. I didn't need to say it.

"It's easy to say words of love and commitment in the bedroom, when no one else will hold you accountable and no sacrifice is required to prove it," Eli said. "In some ways, it's not their fault. As men, our society told us that we were controlled by sexual desire and there's nothing we could do about it. We're merely slaves to our libido and so we must have sex every chance we get. Regardless of what it does to our heart and mind, and if we feel guilt, that is merely our repressive upbringing, not our soul crying out for truth."

The anger of his words made me question, for the first time, Eli's own past.

"It's no better for women," I said. "We're taught that our only worth is our bodies. We are to do anything and everything we can to transform them into what men desire. We are fed lies as girls, that everything we do must be to win a man, and if we are without one, we're worthless." My face flushed with anger.

"You're right," Eli said with a nod. "The culture of porn has taken over—or at least it had. Everything has changed. Sex and babies are no longer separated and the survival of a child will require both parents working together. A year ago, when a father abandoned a child, only the child's life was in danger. Now we've gone back in time and both the mother and the child are at risk. Not of abortion, but of starvation. His selfishness is sentencing two lives to death." Eli spoke with anger and sadness. "Sage is lucky to be with our family. Most women who are pregnant and abandoned by the father probably won't survive, or at least not be able to carry the baby to term, especially during the winter."

"Sage will survive, I'm sure of it," I said.

Eli nodded again. "Sage will survive. Mom and Felicia both say the pregnancy is progressing well, as far as they can tell. Sage feels good, and we have enough to give her the food she needs as her child grows within her."

"But?" I said, hearing the unspoken word.

"But I worry about all the others," he said sadly, his eyes shifting, focusing somewhere far away.

I lowered my head to my knees, my head tilted, staring at my brother's grave. I wondered about all the women who, at this moment, carried a child inside of them, and I prayed they would be strong. I prayed, too, for all the men that, when faced with the choice to live a life of honor or a life of cowardice, they would choose honor.

Twenty-One
EAST

I sat enjoying the stillness, sipping the water Marjorie's daughter had brought me. She was a good-natured child and the same age as Quinn. I avoided her because of it; she reminded me too much of Quinn. But in this last refuge of peace before I left this town, I allowed my gaze to follow her. She ran to her mother and awkwardly tried to pick up her baby brother. Her mother was there to keep them both from tumbling into the dirt.

Marjorie was a good mom, one of the best I'd ever met. And I was blessed to have known many amazing mothers. The best, of course, was my mom. There was nothing like her love for me and all of her kids. Sometimes I think I feel that for Quinn, but then other times I'm sure I don't come close—not to how Marjorie feels for her kids and how my mom feels for me and for Quinn. Some things in my life are totally messed up—"Crosses to bear," as Eli would say—but bad parents isn't one of them. They've always been a consistent source of good in my life. It's why I wanted Quinn to have them for parents instead of me. If they hadn't been who they are, I probably would've tried to parent her myself.

As she was delivered from my body, my mom stayed with me while my dad was handed Quinn. He asked if I wanted to hold her. I turned my head away and cried, the tears of realization that I had to let her go, mixing with the tears of childbirth. The tears of allowing them to take her hurt much more than the tears of her birth.

I was fifteen. I had no choice. They never pushed adoption on me. They offered to help me parent her, to be as involved or not involved as I wanted or needed them to be. But that wasn't right for Quinn. She's their child and has always, for all eternity, been their child. I don't know why the evil of the rape happened, but I know the beauty that came from it.

When they told me her name, I cried out of gratitude and exhaustion. Throughout the pregnancy I was worried my father might struggle with her. I wasn't sure if his love was big enough to love the baby that came from his own baby's rape. I never worried about my mother; she's made to love. She would love Quinn like she loved the rest of her kids. But when he asked me if it was okay to name her after himself … I've never loved my father more than I did at that moment. He fully claimed her as his own, and has never for a second treated her any differently than he treated us—except for spoiling her more than he should.

As an infant, Quinn thrived, while I fell deeper into depression. I held myself together when she was inside of me. She needed me to be strong for her. After her birth, she no longer needed me and I could finally fall apart. My mom begged me to go see the counselor I saw when I first found out I was pregnant, but I refused. She begged me to talk to her and dad, but I refused that too. Sometimes life sucked. No amount of talking was going to change the fact that I had been raped. There were so many nights that I dreamt of him. So many nights I could hear his evil laughter as I cried.

Those memories drove me to train, and to train harder than anyone else at the gym. As I became stronger and fought harder, the fear of the memories faded. I secretly hoped that someday I would see him again, that I would get my revenge, but days turned into years and our paths never crossed. Not for more than a second at a stoplight or from a distance at the grocery store. As I grew stronger he grew weaker—at least, that's how I saw him. When I left for college, I no longer felt the slightest bit of fear toward him or the memory of him.

I felt a prickle of pain on my arm. It was imagined pain as I remembered the knife sliding into my arm, tracing the vein down to my wrist. It didn't hurt. If it had, I might've stopped before the blood started spilling into the tub. I wanted to die. I was so overcome with fear and shame, I felt destroyed and worthless. I wonder why I felt that. Why did I think his sin was mine?

Something about rape is different from all other forms of violence. Trent's soldiers beat me far worse than Mick did, and yet, as my ribs healed I didn't feel my life was no longer worth living. I had no nightmares or flashbacks. No, rape is a different form of violence. It is a spiritual attack as well as physical. Maybe because sex is spiritual as well as physical. I traced the long scar, the very center of the cross, the very center of my cross.

"Everything's about ready," Haz said, stepping beside me.

I shifted my gaze to the present. "Okay," I answered.

"Where were you?" he asked, cocking his head to one side, dimples showing under the stubble.

"I, ah, was remembering something."

"I figured that much," he said, not turning away.

"It wasn't a happy memory," I said, hoping he'd take the hint and leave it alone.

"Does it have to do with your tattoo?"

I rubbed the scar. "Why do you ask?"

"All tattoos tell a story. Yours, I'm guessing, tells an intense one."

"Why are you guessing that?" I asked, trying to make light of his words.

He sat beside me. I turned my arm so he couldn't see the ink.

"It's covering a scar," he said, leaning forward on his elbows and looking back at me with his deep brown eyes. The eyelashes curled up, almost touching his eyelids.

I turned my arm so the crucifix was visible. "Yeah, it is," I said.

"Self-inflicted?"

"Yes," I said, rubbing the scar.

"Yeah, that's sort of what I thought," he said with sadness. "I'm guessing it was something more than a boyfriend breaking up with you or a friend not talking to you."

"I was raped," I said. I wasn't ashamed. It wasn't my sin.

"Somehow I knew that," he said, forcing a smile to hide the pain he felt on my behalf.

"How old were you?" he asked softly.

"Fourteen," I answered.

He flinched on the inside, but didn't allow his face to show it. I could sense it, though. I could sense a lot of things.

"Did you tell anyone?" he asked, trying to keep his voice steady.

"My family."

He nodded his approval. "What happened to the rapist?" he asked, his voice quiet.

"I killed him," I said.

"You did?"

I noticed him flinch. He had not expected that. I would have found his reaction funny were it not for the evil that surrounded this conversation.

"It was after the light, or EMP, or whatever it was. He attacked us, shot Jonah, and killed my grandfather. I fought him, and he died. I hadn't meant to kill him, but I don't feel any guilt. I did right after he died, but soon after that, the guilt left me. I wonder if I should feel guilty. Part of me thinks I should. I ended a life, so I should feel guilt, but I don't." I wondered what he would think of me after he learned I had killed the man who raped me and I felt totally okay about it.

"It sounds like you had no other choice," he said as if he knew what I was thinking.

"I didn't. He had to die and I would rather his blood on my soul than on my dad's or brothers'. He was my demon to battle, not theirs."

"I'm sorry that happened to you," he said, placing a hand over mine. It was a nice gesture, but it made me uncomfortable. Gus was right; he had noticed something I hadn't even realized about myself. Closeness made me uncomfortable; keeping people at a distance felt better, safer.

"Me too," I said, standing. His hand fell away from mine.

John carried his pack. Pam was standing nearby. She was crying and he was trying to console her. He was a good man. She loved him, not in the romantic way, but in the way a person loves the one person who hasn't been taken from you. He cared for her, but to him she was not the last person. In his mind, his family was alive and we were going to find them.

There were times when I found the truth of life overwhelming. This was one of them. John was not a foolish man. He was smarter than most and smarter in ways that actually counted. He understood people and so he must understand that his family was dead. But he did not accept it, and since I believed in hope, I would go with him. And because Haz believed in his city and wanted to return to it, he would go also. We'd search for John's family, but we wouldn't find them. What we would do is learn the city, figure out what was going on—who was controlling what. This knowledge, combined with whatever Jael and Ash discovered at Raven Rock, would help us. Exactly how, none of us knew, but we all agreed it would help.

I lifted my pack. John watched me as I came toward him.

"Happy Fourth of July," Pam said sadly.

I blinked. Was she right? Was today the fourth? It was early July. She must be right.

"Happy Fourth of July," I said back to her as Haz joined us.

Twenty-Two
BRIA

My hands trembled as I stepped down the stairway in my mother's gown. My mother was here on my wedding day; I could feel her presence. It was as if she was physically next to me, though far enough away that she couldn't be seen. I thought back to her journal, to the dream she wrote about soon before she died. She had foreseen this day, as I made my way down the stairs of her grandparents' house. Everyone I loved waited for me outside. She would be beside me every step of the way. Was she holding my brother? Was she holding her grandchild, the one that never had the chance to take its first breath? These thoughts did not hurt; they brought me joy. All those I loved were with me as I gave my life to Jonah.

When I reached the first floor, my friends were there. "You're the most beautiful bride ever," Sage said.

"Thank you," I said, my voice unsteady.

"Are you nervous?" Sara asked.

I nodded.

"Here, have some water," Blaise said from behind me, and handed me a glass.

After gulping all the water, I handed it back to her. "Thank you," I said quietly.

She took the glass from my hand and set it on a step. "I was a thirsty, blushing bride a few months ago. Four, to be exact."

"Is that all it's been?" Sara asked. "It feels like years since your wedding."

"It totally does," Blaise said, with a hint of exhaustion.

It had been a long four months, for all of us.

"It's good, right?" I asked, staring at her. "Marriage, I mean. It's good?"

She adjusted the sleeve of my dress. "So far, my marriage has consisted of my husband and me and our best friends fighting to stay alive, so I'm not sure if I'm the best person to ask. But, I can say so far it has been the most amazing adventure ever."

"Let's hope the first four months of Bria's marriage will be less adventurous than the first four months of yours," Sara said, feigning exhaustion as she handed me the bouquet JP had gathered.

"I'm sure it will be calmer," Blaise said. "How could it not! Are you ready?"

I swallowed the fear I felt, and nodded.

Sara knocked on the door, the signal to tell my father it was time. Blaise opened the front door, the summer sun filling the stone foyer.

Juliette began the wedding song she had mastered on Pops's fiddle, though when she played it, Nonie said it transformed into a violin. Lying down nearby, Astrea watched Juliette's every move. Maria sang, her voice like an angel's. I had come to appreciate her and her family, and not fear them. Her children, Isabelle and Max, sat beside Heath in the back row, Franklin at their feet. The children wiggled in their seats, but far less than I imagined JP wiggled when he was so young.

"We love you," Sara said as she and Sage and Blaise went before me into the yard. Step by step, we passed Richard and Felicia, who sat by themselves in the last row.

Quinn stood beside my father, her basket again overflowing with petals of dozens of different flowers. How beautiful they were. How unique and lovely each one of them was.

"Are you ready?" my father asked as he extended his left arm.

His eyes were already swimming with tears. My mother had been right: my father was crying on my wedding day and knowing the real him, it was expected. He had become a good and kind man. He was the first to go without food if ever there wasn't enough and the last to complain about the physical demands of our life.

"I am," I said.

Blaise was right. This was the greatest adventure I would ever go on.

Though my father's limp had not lessened, his quiet strength steadied me as we made our way toward the kitchen table that today sat in the middle of the yard and was transformed into an altar for our wedding Mass.

From the side of the house, Fulton and Talin ran and then stopped when they saw us, as if the horses hadn't meant to interrupt. Everyone chuckled at their abrupt arrival and even more abrupt stop. As I laughed I found Jonah. Our eyes locked. His filled with tears—something I had not expected, though I did not fear them. They were not of sadness or regret; they were of gratitude. I felt the same, but my eyelashes were darkened with mascara and I would not have black streaks running down my face on my wedding day.

He wore a baby-blue tie over his crisp white shirt, which pulled tight across his chest and shoulders. His jeans were stained but not ripped. His hair was as short as it had been on the day we met, his face smoothly shaven. He had never been more handsome.

It had been only eight months since that first night on the highway, but it felt like an eternity. We both had changed so much since then. Physically, of course—our bodies stronger and more muscular—but emotionally and spiritually also. We had wounds that needed to heal, and they had.

My heart beat faster as I realized I was walking toward my destiny. I was walking toward the man who would be mine for the rest of my life and I would be his. As scary as that thought of surrender had once been, I couldn't wait—to be his forever.

JP stood beside Jonah. He was rocking up and down on his tiptoes, bouncing without technically moving. I knew, without looking, that Charlotte was trying to signal for him to stop. I loved them both. She was a wonderful example of a mother and a wife, and he was one of the most amazing kids ever. They had told me he cried a lot while we were gone, and he still occasionally cried for East, but he was so alive and energetic. He would never have done well in a school where he was compelled to sit still all day. Here, in this world where more energy meant more crops planted and animals skinned, it was a gift.

Quinn reached her youngest brother and stuck her tongue out at him before taking her place beside Sara. She had gone from reserved and shy, to ornery. Charlotte said it was a phase, that East had gone through it too and it would pass. In my opinion, the orneriness never really left East, though I kept that to myself.

Blaise and Josh were on opposite ends of the altar, making eyes at one another. I wondered if this reminded them of their wedding day and the love they shared for one another.

Jonah stepped forward, reaching a hand toward me, taking my hand from my father. It was an old custom, but one my father had insisted on.

We turned to face the altar and Eli.

"Who gives this beautiful woman to my undeserving little brother?" Eli said.

"Eli!" Charlotte said with a gasp, and I understood then, that orneriness was a family trait.

"I do and her mother does too," my father said, tears streaming down his sunken cheeks.

My mother's journal was right; he was far too thin. I hugged him and Jonah hugged him. My father had done a lot wrong in his life, yet he had found me, rescued me, and tried a dozen times to bring me back to the faith—that didn't work—but, it was done out of love, and I loved being loved by him. I was grateful to have my true father back.

He limped to his seat beside Charlotte. Like at Blaise's wedding, they would be crying both for the beauty of the ceremony as well as missing my mom and, now, East. Quint sat between his wife and his mother, looking proud at the sons he had raised. He was, for me, the best example of a father there was, and as I turned back to Jonah I found myself so grateful to Quint and Charlotte for raising the man I was marrying.

Jonah's hand held mine, his fingers rough and calloused. I would want them no other way. This was how his hand had always felt in mine and I loved it. He worked hard—harder than Eli or Josh—and I admired him for that.

"You're so beautiful," he whispered, his eyes bloodshot with tears.

I wiped his cheeks with my free hand, and he leaned into it as I had the first night we'd spent in this place. I'd been afraid then … afraid to allow him to love me. I was no longer afraid. He kissed the palm of my hand.

"Ah-hmm," uttered Eli, pretending to clear his throat. "Mom's right. This is not a joking occasion, but it is a joyful one. Every sacramental marriage is the uniting of two souls in a way that I don't think any of us can fully understand, or at least I can't. You two are blessed in a way that so many are not. You have, among your parents and grandparents, the examples of healthy, loving marriages. Jonah and I had that growing up, in Mom and Dad and in Nonie and Pops. It was clear even on the bad days, and there were many—and there will be many for you two—that even on those days there was a grace that came from the sacrament of their marriage."

I shuddered at the thought of all Quint and Charlotte had been through. It was so much, and yet, there they sat holding one another, madly in love, as they witnessed the first of their children getting married. I prayed that Jonah and I would be so blessed.

After casting a glance at all those we loved, Eli said, "Often, we think of the world in black-and-white. We see the concrete, the scientific, and we fail to think beyond that. We fail to understand that while the physical world around us is good—yes, even in its current state it is good—there is still more to our existence. As Christians, we believe this world is good and important. But that it is a mere stepping-off point for our eternal life, and *that* life is the goal. It is that life that we spend this life preparing for, and it is through our vocations that this preparation takes place most concretely.

"My brother once thought he was called to the vocation of the priesthood. While it is a noble vocation and one I am blessed to be called to, it is not his. It never was. He has always been called to marriage and more specifically, to you, Bria."

I blushed at the thought of Jonah having always been called to me. It seemed impossible and absolute at the same time.

"You, Bria, are his vocation, just as you, Jonah, are Bria's vocation. It is through your marriage that you will feel most clearly God's love and trials. There is no love without sacrifice, and on this day you must each die to yourself and place the other person before you. While this is an important truth for Bria, and all brides, I believe it to be even more true for Jonah, and all grooms. They are called to be like Christ, to offer their bodies for their brides. They are called to sacrifice in a way that an unmarried man like myself will never fully understand."

"Amen to that!" Josh joked from beside Jonah.

I turned to see Blaise glaring at him.

Quint laughed too loudly, and Charlotte and Nonie both elbowed him. My father's head was bowed in reverence.

What he wouldn't have given to sacrifice for my mother. How short his time was with her.

"It is a truth," Eli said, "a truth that we joke about, but a truth nonetheless. Married women sacrifice. I do not deny that, especially the one married to my brother." Eli and Josh both laughed. "But there is something about women that allows this sacrifice to come more fully and more easily. Certainly, I speak in generalities, but on the whole, men struggle most in marriages, to learn and understand who they are in relation to their wives and children. Men struggle most with selfishness that does not allow them to see their wives as someone they give to, rather than take from. Jonah, you have always been giving, but you have always been selfish. I say this not to hurt you but to love you. Bria, while you struggled so long to see yourself as worthy, you have been worthy all along. Your heart is pure, so very pure, and I understand clearly why my brother began falling in love with you the instant he saw you on that deserted highway. Sacrifice will be easy for you, but you must allow Jonah to walk beside you. You must allow him to sacrifice and give as well, or you will be withholding from him a key part of his vocation and you will both suffer."

I would give my life for Jonah and he would do the same for me. Eli knew this, yet he called on Jonah to sacrifice more and me to sacrifice less. This, I did not understand.

217

"Together, the two of you will create a family. Perhaps there will be biological children or adopted children, perhaps not. Perhaps you will live to celebrate sixty-three years of marriage, as Nonie and Pops did, perhaps not. Perhaps you will always be madly in love, perhaps you will not. Life is uncertain, especially given the current state of the world, but what you are doing today is permanent. The two of you will be bound together through this life and the next, in a way that I do not understand but know to be true. I say all of this to scare you just a little,"—he offered me a hint of a smile—"to make sure you are in fact aware that what you are committing to today is not the stuff of fairy tales, it is not about happily ever after. It is about real life, real struggles, real disagreements, and real love. It will not be easy … but it will be worth it.

"There. I've said far more than my share. This is not my wedding. This is yours and this sacrament is not about me, it is about you two and God. I am merely here to facilitate and I am honored to do that.

"Nonie, please come forward so we may listen to the first reading."

Nonie stood and made her way toward us. With tears in her eyes, she took the Bible from Eli. She had chosen this Scripture verse on her own. I tried to hear the words, but I couldn't; my mind was racing with the awareness of what Jonah and I were agreeing to.

Eli had explained yesterday at the rehearsal that this verse from the beginning of the Bible represented the beginning of society and how the marriage relationship must be prioritized and made first, above parents and above children. In this moment—when it was the two of us professing our desire to spend our lives together—that was easy to do. However, Eli had cautioned there would be times in life when other relationships might try to take precedence. We would need to guard against that, not in a selfish way but in a life-giving way. Marriage, he had said, was the building block of families and society. It must be continually strengthened and protected.

After her reading, Nonie stood in front of us and kissed me on the cheek before returning to her seat beside Quint. Charlotte nudged JP, who sat in front of her. He stood and came toward us. He wrapped his arms around me and gave me a quick hug before continuing on to where Eli stood, holding the Bible for him. JP read loud and clear, like he had practiced.

The words from Corinthians, which Eli said practically everyone read at a wedding, washed over me. They were good words. Words that reminded me how to love and how not to love. Even before I believed in God, I would have appreciated these words.

JP returned to his seat, his parents both placing a hand on his shoulder. His mother leaned forward, whispering that he had done a good job.

Behind us, Eli stood and Jonah took my hand to signal me to stand.

Eli said, "A reading from the Gospel according to Matthew."

"Praise to you, Lord Jesus Christ." The words came from all around me.

That was one of the strangest things about Catholics. Everything they said and did at Mass was scripted. Even at their young ages, JP and Quinn had memorized the script. They often didn't do it, but when their parents glared at them they followed along, sitting and standing or kneeling and speaking with everyone else. It was like watching a choreographed production. The strangest part was I was starting to learn the choreography.

Eli had completed the reading. This happened to me often: my mind drifted and before I realized it they had moved on to the next part. Jonah pulled my hand and I sat beside him.

"I cannot think of a more fitting Gospel reading than one that speaks of the Light of the world, when we are all here today,"—he raised his hands to indicate the yard and house—"because of a great light that changed the world. The light we all experienced last Thanksgiving changed our world, but the

Light the world experienced two thousand years ago also changed the world, and if I may be so bold, in a way greater than an EMP could ever do. Through marriage, you two are being asked to also change the world for the better. It is tempting, really tempting, to focus only on ourselves and our family, and while that is where we must begin, to ensure we are strong and our family is strong, that is not the end. Jesus is saying in this reading that we are all, each of us, called to be a light for the world. We cannot hide our proverbial lights under a basket. We must allow them to shine and be seen. We must allow them to go out into the world and shed light in the darkness. That is what we are each called to do, and that is what you two are agreeing to do together for the rest of your lives.

"And so, I ask, are you both prepared to follow the path of marriage, wherever it may lead you?"

Jonah stood and I stood beside him. "I am," Jonah and I said together.

My mind raced in fear. He took my hand in his, and my mind eased. With him beside me, I could do this. I could make this commitment and keep my promise to him.

"Are you both open to the possibility of children and the blessings and challenges,"—he winked at JP—"that they bring?"

"I am," we said in unison.

Though the thought of being a mother brought immense fear, I did not want to live my life in fear. Jonah understood my fears and together we would discern when or if we would try to conceive.

"Please join your right hands. ... Jonah, do you take Bria to be your wife, to love her and support her, to honor her and respect her, no matter what may come, forsaking all others, this day and all the days of your life?"

Jonah squeezed my hand and, his forehead almost touching mine, said softly, "I do."

How did I get so lucky?

"Bria, do you take Jonah to be your husband and partner in all things? To be faithful to him and turn away from all others? To be with him always, in sickness and in health, in safety and in threat, this day and all the days of your life?"

"I do," I said, the words coming out as a whisper.

"May the Lord, in his kindness, strengthen the consent you have declared before the Church and graciously bring to fulfillment his blessings within you. What God has joined, let no one tear apart.

"John Paul, may I have the rings?"

"Rings?" I said in surprise.

Jonah grinned.

JP stepped forward, pulling from his pocket two rings, and handing them to Eli.

Eli held them and blessed them, saying: "Bless, O Lord, these rings which we bless in your name. So that those who wear them may remain entirely faithful to each other, abide in peace and in your will, and live always in mutual charity. Through Christ our Lord."

"Amen," Jonah said, and I added, "Amen."

Eli handed the first ring to Jonah.

Jonah said to me, "This was your mom's. My mom had been saving it for you, for your wedding day." He slipped the ring on my finger. The cool metal slid perfectly in place. It was simple, no diamond, no decoration, just two carved lines in a band of gold.

I turned.

Charlotte was crying, Quint's arm around her, supporting her. On her other side, my father cried as he held her hand. My hand trembled as I thought of how much she loved my mother, how much she loved me. I released Jonah's hand and went to her.

"Thank you," I said as I wrapped my arms around her.

"Your mom would be so happy," Charlotte said. "This was her dream. We joked about it when you were born and it's what we both sincerely prayed for. I never thought it would happen." More tears fell as she undoubtedly thought of my mother's death, my father stealing me away, and the world turning upside down. "But I kept praying." She sniffed.

"Thank you for praying for me and for loving me, and my mother," I said.

Her arms tightened and then released me.

I turned and went back to Jonah.

"And this, Bria, is for Jonah," Eli said, handing me a ring of braided copper.

"How did you make this?" I said, in amazement at its humble beauty.

"Your dad helped me," Jonah said. "We used some copper wiring and braided it, and heated it so it melted and we smoothed the inside."

I examined it more closely. He was right. The braided copper circled the outside, and the underside was smooth.

"It's beautiful," I said, slipping it onto his finger, "just like you." I squeezed his hands. I had never expected to have rings, but I never expected to have Jonah, either. I wondered about the prayers of my mother and Charlotte. Had they brought us together? Had they been part of the creation of this moment?

"You two are officially husband and wife," Eli said. "You may kiss your husband," he said, winking at me.

Jonah stepped toward me. I lifted my hand to his clean-shaven face. Our lips connected with an unexpected intensity. Yes, there was passion, but there had always been passion. Even our first kiss, when Jonah was drugged, was passionate. This was something more, something I could not explain.

Our friends erupted into applause and I remembered they were there. I pulled away from Jonah, his hand in mine.

He guided me to our seats. Jonah had asked if our wedding could include a Mass, and I saw no reason not to do this.

My mind again drifted to the ring on my finger. Jonah's hand was laced in mine. We were married. It was real. My mother's dream had come true.

Eli stood in front of us, offering Jonah the Eucharist. Jonah received it with reverence. Eli gave me a blessing. Everyone else came behind us in single file to either receive the Eucharist or a blessing. The organization of this process always impressed me.

Jonah knelt in the dirt and bowed his head. I watched him, no longer trying to hide that I was doing so. I admired so much about him, most of all his humility. Though he was healthy and the strongest of us, he bowed his head to someone greater than him. This had been so strange to me in the beginning, so different than how I was raised and how I had existed in the world. Jonah sat after Eli took a seat for a moment of quiet prayer.

When Eli stood, everyone else stood. "The Mass has ended. Let us go in peace and celebration."

Twenty-Three
BRIA

Our wedding meal was a feast like none of us had eaten in months. It was JP's contribution that I was most grateful for. He had found us a beehive and a blackberry patch. Both had been used to make our wedding dessert, the most amazing blackberry cobbler I'd ever eaten.

Metal clinked against glass. Josh stood at the center of our gathering. "I'm the best man, only because Eli was already the celebrant, but still, it counts. And since I'm the best man, I have the privilege of making the first toast. So here it goes. Bria, I've known you for, I guess, three years, and in that time I can honestly say I've only liked you for like a year or a year and a half. Ouch!" Blaise had elbowed him.

"Hey!" I said.

"Yeah, that sounds mean. Sorry about that, but the thing is, it's true." He jumped out of the way as Blaise made another jab at him.

"What? You know she drove me crazy," he said to Blaise.

My mouth open, I couldn't decide if I should be hurt or shocked or amused.

"But … but,"—he said, holding his hand out to block his wife—"I like you now, and I always liked the real you before, but I almost never saw that person. Every once in a while, I'd catch a glimpse of the real you and I'd tell Blaise how great you were, and she'd say, 'See, that's who she really is. That's why I love her.' But then you'd hide again and you became someone I tolerated but didn't like. As we spent more and more time together, the real you started showing up more and more, and then the world imploded and you couldn't hide anymore. And as stupid as it sounds, that has been the best thing that ever happened to you."

I thought about his words. Millions died. Some in an instant, some starved slowly over time. Others, like Faith, died months later. Millions more were likely to die in the near future and I might be one of them. Perhaps it would be Sage as she struggled to give birth. This must have been the largest loss of human life the world had ever seen. But for me and my own little life, the world's imploding brought me my husband and my father. It brought me truth and family and love and freedom. Yes, in a weird way, Josh was right.

With his glass raised, Josh continued, "Now you are yourself and someone I love, and you just married someone else I love, though when I first met him, I thought he was going to eat us."

Jonah cocked his head and scrunched his eyebrows in confusion.

Sara and I laughed. Blaise sat in defeat, shielding her eyes with a hand. She was trying to appear upset, but I could tell she was giggling.

"You thought I was going to eat you?" Jonah asked, saying the words slowly and clearly.

"Yeah, it was the middle of the night, we were stranded. You and East showed up to rescue us. It seemed too coincidental."

Jonah stared at him in confusion. Eli and JP were laughing so hard they could barely breathe.

"That's not the point," Josh said. "The point is that from the beginning, you were yourself, and after the fear of being eaten subsided, I was amazed by your goodness. You and your family took us in, you fed us, you sheltered us, we wouldn't have survived without you. And all of that was great, but you were also kind and honest. Watching you and your family, I couldn't help but think of the first Christians. They were in a world defined by violence and fear, and yet they sacrificed for strangers.

"Again, we're in a world of violence and fear. A world where survival of the fittest is being spouted as a way to make our nation great. We took it for granted before—or at least I did—that people of all faiths or no faith would be kind and helpful to strangers. It was the American way. We protected the weak. That is no longer the American way, or not the way of those who are currently in command of our nation's capital. Thank God. Literally, thank you, God, that your family didn't believe that way, or we would have been toast. You wouldn't have eaten us—that is pretty gross—but you certainly wouldn't have taken food from your own mouths to feed us. You wouldn't have taken clothing and supplies from those you loved and given them to strangers.

"I guess my rambling is to say I've respected you from almost as soon as I met you, Jonah, and I don't think there's a better woman in the world for you, now that she's who she actually is."

Blaise pulled him down as she stood up. "I think what my husband was trying to say was that you two are great. We love you and we wish you nothing but happiness."

Everyone clapped as she sat down.

"That's what I said," Josh said from beside her.

"Okay, sweetie, if you say so," she said, kissing him on the cheek.

Sara stood up. "As the maid of honor, I go next." She cleared her throat. "Bria, you and I became friends because we were both afraid of the truth, the truth of who we were, the truth of what the world was. You and I, we hid from the truth. That's what started our friendship, but it's your amazingness that made it grow. Josh may not have seen it, but I totally did. You have always been the kindest and most giving person. You remember that day when you literally gave me the shirt off your back?"

I laughed at the memory. "I did have others," I said.

"Yeah, but that's not the point. You always understood what it meant to be a friend. You did anything and everything you could for me and Blaise, and you never talked about us or hurt us in any way. I was not used to that and it's one of the reasons I love you so much. And, one of the many reasons you and Jonah are meant for each other and are going to be so happy. When we met, you were lost. I was too, but even when you were lost, you were good to your core."

I opened my mouth to object.

She raised a hand to stop me. "You made some awful decisions, I get that. I have too, but that's not the point. The point is you were made for great love and you have found it. Jonah is everything you have ever deserved and you are everything he has deserved, and I am so happy for you both."

I went to her and hugged her. We pulled Blaise into our hug. "I love you two so much," I said so my father couldn't hear. "You were my family when I had none."

"And now you are surrounded by family," Blaise said, "and I could not be happier for you."

Our hug continued until I saw my father stand. I released my friends as he came toward me.

"I never expected this day to be so hard," he said, tears welling in his eyes. "You look so much like your mom." He choked as he buried his face against my shoulder, his back rocking as he cried.

Quint came to him and placed a hand on his back.

My father sniffed and pulled away from me, taking my hand in his. "When your mom died," he said, "I lost all sense of who I was. She had been my world. People say that all the time, but with us it was true. Even today, I can still feel her with me. There were many nights that I would dream of her and wake up sobbing, remembering that she was gone and so was our son."

Tears streamed down both our faces.

Jonah drew near me and placed a hand on my back. Nonie handed me a handkerchief. I dabbed at the black mascara streaking down my face.

My father said, "I couldn't look at you without seeing her, and so my solution was to stop seeing you. I stayed away, worked harder. I told myself it was for you, but it wasn't. As the years passed, my heart hardened and my hatred for God"—he choked on the word—"grew. I was everything you did not deserve, and I am so sorry. And I'm sorry to make your wedding a time for my confession." He shook his head in frustration. "That's not what I meant to do. I came up here to tell you how beautiful you are and how proud I am of you, though I take no credit for the woman you are. That was your mom, loving you, praying for you, watching over you from above. She loves you, sweetheart, and she never ever stopped. I sense her with me most days, but today it is so strong." He sniffed. "I keep expecting to see her or feel her hand in mine." He turned away and took a deep, calming breath.

"She is so proud of you and she has every right to be. I love you, honey, and I pray you will have the happiness your mom and I had—but for decades longer." He was crying as Quint led him back to his seat and Charlotte came toward me.

She wiped my face with the handkerchief. "He loves you so much, and so do Quint and I." She kissed me on the cheek and then rose to her tiptoes and kissed her son on the cheek. "This is an answer to our prayers. Your dad is right. I give your mom all the credit," she said, hugging me before returning to her seat.

"All right, that was kind of a lot," Eli said from behind us. "I declare the saying of deeply heartfelt sentiments part of the reception over. It is time for dancing, more eating, and general merriment!"

"Thank you," I mouthed to him as Juliette picked up the violin and began a song that reminded me of something that actually would be played on a fiddle. Astrea stretched her paws and rolled over onto her side.

"May I have the honor of this dance, Mrs. Page?" Jonah asked, bowing like they would have a hundred years ago.

I curtseyed. "Why, certainly, Mr. Page."

Our families clapped as we began to twirl on the dance floor. I had taken ballroom dancing as a child and though I was technically not supposed to lead him, I was leading him and he was doing a great job matching my motions. Quinn giggled and pulled Isabelle onto the dance floor, which was the center of our gathering space and decorated with wildflowers. Isabelle and Quinn copied us. Soon the rest of the family was up. Sara asked my father and Sage asked Eli; they, along with Nonie and JP and the other married couples, danced beside us. The song finished and Juliette played another piece. I was sure Pops was playing along from above. Dancing to the even faster pace made my face flush. When it ended, Jonah signaled to Blaise, who kissed Josh and came toward us.

"I have a surprise for you," Jonah said to me, his eyes twinkling in the late afternoon sun.

"You do? What is it?"

"I'm going to show you, but first, go with Blaise," he said as Blaise appeared and took my hand.

"Come on." She laughed as she pulled me toward the house.

I followed, glancing behind me before I entered. The others were watching, but I saw only Jonah. As I disappeared into the house, Quinn was pulling him onto the dance floor.

I climbed the stairs, trying to keep up with Blaise. "Where are we going?"

"Upstairs, to get you changed," she said.

"Changed?"

"Yes, this is our one wedding dress and we can't have you ruining it."

"What makes you think I would ruin it?"

Her smile broadened as she shut the door. "Here, let me help you unlace it," she said.

I turned my back to her. "What's the surprise?" I asked, my voice sounding more scared and less excited than I'd intended.

The wedding was over and so was the reception. Only one thing was left, the wedding night, and though that was one of the main reasons I had agreed to marry so quickly, I found myself unbelievably nervous.

As Blaise finished untying the dress, she said, "I can't tell you. But don't worry, it will be wonderful."

She helped me out of the dress and already had jeans and an ironed button-down shirt laid out for me. The shirt was my mom's—elegant and modest. The jeans also were hers. They weren't worn down to shreds, like most of our clothes.

"What's it like?" I asked as I finished dressing and she hung the gown.

She lifted her eyes to mine. "You know," she said, blushing.

"But I don't, not really, not with someone I love, someone I'm … married to." I flopped onto the bed.

She sat beside me. "Are you nervous?" she asked, smoothing my hair. It was pulled into a tight bun at the back of my head; the style hid my scar. Usually I wore my hair in a ponytail, but that had seemed too casual for my wedding.

"Yes," I confessed.

"You love him, you trust him, and you should. He's amazing," she said, coming up beside me.

"People thought Trent was amazing too," I said, fighting back the tears.

"Bria, he's not Trent, or any other guy. He's Jonah, and he loves you more than he loves his own life. He doesn't want to take from you, he wants to be your helper and supporter throughout life. And he will respect you one hundred percent in all areas of life, that one included. If you aren't ready, tell him. He will be okay with that."

"I was ready. I mean really ready. But now ...." I shook my hands, trying to calm down. "It's a lot of pressure."

"It's not, though. He's not pressuring you and he won't," she said, clasping my right hand. She chuckled.

"Don't laugh," I said, feeling hurt.

"It's funny. I freaked out before my wedding and you're freaking out after. Poor Sara, she's doomed to be a mess the whole time."

"Or," I said, "she'll be totally calm throughout the whole thing."

"Knowing her, she will be," Blaise said, squeezing my hand. "Come on, he's going to worry you got stuck in your dress or something."

"Okay," I said, following her from the room.

"Breathe," she said as we made our way down the stairs.

I sucked in air, unaware until I did so, that I needed to.

We stepped outside and Jonah was there on top of Fulton. Talin stood beside them, her saddle decorated with wildflowers.

A broad smile crossed my face. "Where are we going?" I asked as I nuzzled Talin.

She pawed at the ground in excitement as I swung myself onto her saddle.

"It's a surprise," he said, handing me her reins.

Our friends and family gathered around us. "Have fun, you two," Josh said, winking at me.

My face turned crimson. Blaise elbowed him hard in the stomach.

"Ready?" Jonah asked.

I nodded. He gave Fulton a squeeze with his legs and the horse began to trot. I did the same with Talin. Soon we were galloping and we could no longer see our friends. Being on Talin made me forget my concerns. We rode straight ahead for a while and then turned back toward our house and family.

"Where are we going?" I asked again.

"Not far. We could've walked, but I thought you'd appreciate time with Talin," Jonah said.

"You're right," I said in wonder. I was overwhelmed by all he had done to prepare for this day that marked the beginning of our life together.

We were in the woods, following the path to the old spring house. We hardly ever came this way; with no surplus food to refrigerate, we had no reason to.

My mouth fell open when I saw that a room had been built onto the spring-cooled house.

"We're here," Jonah said as he swung his leg over Fulton and hopped off. He tied the reins to a post. I went to slide off Talin and Jonah caught me. He kissed me as he swung me around. I loved the feeling of being in his arms.

"I love you," I whispered.

He set my feet onto the forest floor. "I love you too," he said, kissing me softly.

I wrapped my arms around his neck. He bent down and lifted me back into the air.

"What're you doing?"

"Carrying you over the threshold," he said.

I slipped Talin's reins over the post as he opened the homemade door to the room. He took two steps inside, with me in his arms. It was dim and the floor was dirt. The room was furnished with a bed, a wooden table, and two chairs. A glass jar overflowing with wildflowers sat in the center of the table. A quilt covered the bed and pillows.

238

"What do you think?" he asked as he allowed my feet to touch the ground.

"You built this?" I asked in amazement.

"I had help, but it was mostly me. Sara put the wildflowers here. She said it added a feminine touch. And the quilt was your mom's. Your dad thought you would like it." His hand held mine as he watched me take it all in.

"It's perfect," I said as I hugged him. "You're perfect." I raised my head so that our lips touched.

He kissed me and gradually moved his lips to my neck. He moved his hands, slowly unbuttoning the bottom of my shirt. His hand felt hot against my stomach, and I realized how right this felt and how different it felt from all the times before.

I wished I was like Blaise or Jonah and had nothing to compare this to.

"Are you okay?" he asked with concern, and I realized I was crying.

I pressed my face to his neck. "I'm sorry, sorry things aren't … different. That my past isn't different."

He wrapped his arms around me and exhaled a soft breath. "Let me love you," he whispered.

I held him tighter. "Thank you for loving me," I said, kissing his neck.

He slid the bobby pins from my hair and the bun fell. His fingers grazed the scar as he loosened my hair. My body tensed.

"I love you," he said. "Every part of you, even the parts you wish were different."

He kissed me and my past disappeared. I was here with him and nowhere else, with no one else. This was the beginning—*he* was the beginning.

"You're so incredible," I said.

I loosened his tie and unbuttoned his shirt. He took off the tie and tossed it onto the back of a chair. My hands pressed against his chest and slid around to his back, holding him close to me.

"Is this what you want?" he asked, his eyes staring deeply into mine as if trying to read a hidden message. "We can wait."

"Don't you think we've waited long enough?" I asked, teasing.

"I just … it's important to me that this is right for you. That this is what you want."

I could hear his nervousness.

I moved my hands back to his chest and traced the rosary tattoo that encircled the scar from Mick's bullet. "Jonah, *you* are what I want, now and forever," I said, stepping my body into his. His arms relaxed around my shoulders as I slid the shirt from his back.

Twenty-Four
EAST

"The fires were here too," Haz said in a way that reminded me how much he loved this city.

"This wasn't burned when we flew over," John said, concern in his voice. "It happened later."

"The fires on the south end burned for months," Haz said. "It was probably the same here."

Entering the city from the north was easier than the south. There were no rivers or walls to keep us in or out. The few guards were stationed only at the roads. We slipped between houses and entered unnoticed. Once we were in, it was easy enough to move in the shadows.

It felt better to be sneaking into the city, rather than trying to escape from it. An offensive position was always better than defensive. It allowed for clearer thought and more intentional actions.

John remained hopeful, but only in his mind. When he spoke of his family, his hope faded and depression threatened to engulf him. So he did not speak of them. I didn't blame him. If the person I loved and our two teenage kids had watched someone drag me away eight months ago, I wouldn't be able to speak about them, either. I'd want to believe they were alive, but to actually speak about them and, by doing so, bring them into the world we were in, that would be difficult. John did, at least, tell us the location of his apartment. We would start there, like we had done with Sara's family.

We stood, hiding in the shadows of a mostly burned building, waiting for a squadron of troops to pass.

Haz signaled for us to move forward. I followed John. He didn't fit into this world and I felt the need to protect him. Perhaps being imprisoned for so long kept him from adapting to the concrete finality of our world. Though it seemed as if he was from a different time: when leather-bound books were read and grand pianos were played. If the United States was a monarchy, I would have sworn he was from its aristocracy. Momma Pryce was right: he never would have survived the search for his family without us.

Haz was leading us toward the White House. It was his goal to get us as close as possible so we could learn as much as we could. We stopped. Guns fired to the south of us. The sound of their bullets echoed down the streets. By the time the sound reached our ears, it was nothing more than pop … pop … pop.

A moment later there was more firing.

"Someone is returning fire," Haz said.

I listened; he was right. Those guns sounded different; the type of weapon was different and so was the direction. Someone was fighting back.

Hope surged within me—maybe others were already fighting for our freedom … and the fate of our country did not actually rest on us.

We waited in silence as the pops continued to echo down the street. After they'd stopped, Haz signaled for us to move forward. The route he was taking us on was more directly south. He was curious and so was I.

The buildings around us were intact; the fires had not been here. We stood in the alley of a brick building. All the buildings here were either brick or stone. No wonder they were intact. Even if a fire had started inside one of them, it wouldn't have escaped. I raised my head. Even the roofs were still there.

Haz stopped at a two-story office building. The doors were made of heavy wood. We were near the White House. This building must have been worth a fortune before the light. Haz bent over, inspecting something. There was a single spot of what appeared to be red paint in the corner of the door, near the shallow brick step. I doubted anyone would have noticed it if they weren't searching for it.

I wondered why he was looking for it.

"I think we should try this door," Haz said, keeping his voice low.

"Why?" I asked.

"When my dad and I were trying to escape from Trent and his murderers, someone helped us. It wasn't enough to save my dad or the antibiotics, but it was enough to save me," he said.

"And this is the door?" I asked incredulously.

"No," Haz said. "That was on the other side of the city, but the door the person came out of had the same red paint."

"And you think it's a signal."

"I doubt this paint was here before the EMP," Haz said.

The thought of anything being out of place on the buildings around here was amusing. "Yeah. Not in this part of town."

"We agree to try the door?" Haz said, his hand on the handle.

I nodded. John didn't reply, which I took as acceptance but not an endorsement.

Haz drew his gun. Mine was already in my hand. He twisted the handle and the door opened. In front of us, carpeted stairs were stained with mud and to the side were glass double doors. These doors were clean; they had not been entered by the person with muddy shoes.

I whispered, "The second floor offers more protection."

Haz nodded. He pushed his back to the wall as he climbed the stairs. I went up, against the other wall. John stayed behind us. As we rounded a corner of the staircase landing, Haz went first. I waited for his signal and joined him against the far wall. We were visible from above. Shadows moved, and we pointed our guns.

"Stop!"

It was a child's voice, coming from above us.

"We don't want to hurt anyone," Haz called out. "We're only hoping for information."

"Why should we believe you?" Another child, a girl, said from beside the boy who had first spoken.

"You have no reason to trust us other than our word," John said, his arms raised as he moved from the shadows, into the sunlight that illuminated the staircase from the windows above.

It was a daring move, one that put him in danger. From where we stood we wouldn't be able to stop him from being shot. The children spoke in hurried tones to one another.

"Put your guns away and your hands up," the girl said. "And slowly come up the stairs."

John didn't hesitate, and I wondered if it was bravery or stupidity that caused him to act so brashly. We complied. Haz went first, to protect me. With our guns at our hips and hands up, we climbed the stairs.

As we stepped onto the second floor, six guns pointed at us. Other young people stood behind those six. They also were armed, though with knives and pipes. They were all young, younger than me and far younger than Haz and John. They wore similar clothing—slave clothes, as Haz had called it when we met Juliette.

"What do you want?" a girl with braided red hair asked.

"We're hoping for a place to stay for the night, and for information if you have it." Haz had adjusted his voice so it sounded kinder and softer, less threatening than normal.

A boy in a black T-shirt said, "Who are you?"

"My name is Haz. This is East. And this is John."

"I meant what side are you on," the boy said, irritated to repeat himself.

"We've been away," Haz said. "We weren't aware there were sides until an hour or so ago, when we heard the return fire."

The kids—teenagers, really, only a few years younger than me—glanced at one another as if trying to figure out if anyone could be so unaware of life in this city as we said.

"Sit over there," the girl with the braid said, directing us with a wave of her gun.

We went to the corner and sat. I didn't like being on the floor with people standing around us, but Haz and I could disarm most of them before they understood we were attacking. The few we couldn't disarm before they had a chance to fire, would likely miss and ... we wouldn't. It was a mistake for them to allow us to keep our guns, a mistake I was thankful they made.

"You said there are sides," Haz said, still with a calm voice. "What sides?"

His hands moved slowly to his lap. John and I did the same.

"Why should we tell you?" the girl with the braid said.

The boy in the black shirt said, "Come on, Amber, what difference does it make? It's not like it's a secret."

"Whatever, Xander, it's a free country. Tell them if you want to," she said, irritated.

John said, "Is it still a free country?"

"That's what we're fighting for," the boy, Xander, said.

Another boy, with shoulder-length hair and a thin mustache, said, "Yeah, but no one else is."

"Please," Amber said, annoyed. "There's a ton of us. We just hide better than the other sides."

"Okay, so your side is the freedom side?" Haz asked, redirecting them to his question.

"Yeah," Xander said, "and the two other sides are the government and the rebellion."

"How is your side different than the rebellion?" I asked, trying to soften my voice like Haz had done.

Amber exhaled in annoyance and spoke. "We are for a free country. The government side wants to control everything. Everything. It's weird, and the rebellion ... they aren't any better. I mean, they say they are, but they aren't. So those of us who simply want the freedom to do what we want have joined together, and we're doing what we can to stay alive and keep either side from getting too much power."

"So, in other words, you're doing what you can to sabotage both sides?" Haz said, chuckling. "That's impressive."

"It's not that impressive," Xander said. "There's so much fighting within the ranks of both sides, they mostly implode. We give them a push every once in a while," he said, not bothering to suppress a smile.

John asked, "How do you sabotage them?"

"We have our ways," the boy with the thin mustache said. "But there's no reason to share that with you." He winked at Amber, who was visibly irritated that they were speaking to us at all.

"That's good," Haz said. "It's good to share some information, but not all. That's wise."

I leaned my back against the wall. It had taken us two full days of hiking to get here, and it felt good to sit in relative safety. This building—aside from the dab of red paint—was nondescript and from the outside appeared deserted. Some of the windows were broken out but not all; it was enough to make it look like every other building. These freedom fighters were not a threat to us.

The windows were darkening; twilight was beginning to fall.

"May we stay here for the night?" I asked, trying to sound nonthreatening.

"You're welcome to guard us," Haz added, "and we promise not to hurt you."

Xander laughed. "We aren't worried about you hurting us," he said.

He was prideful, too prideful for this world. He would get himself and others he cared about hurt.

"What do you think, Amber?" the boy with the mustache asked thoughtfully.

All eyes turned to Amber.

"Fine, but someone is going to guard them all night and it's not going to be me," she said. She folded her arms across her chest in a dramatic, aggravated way.

Twenty-Five
BRIA

Morning light filled our room. I moved my fingers across Jonah's chest, from one tattoo to the other. It seemed like so long ago when we met, but the pink skin of his scar reminded me it had been only months.

He opened his eyes. "Good morning," he said in a tired voice.

"How did this happen so quickly?" I asked, my fingers grazing his chest.

"You and me?" He pulled me closer.

I liked that he could understand my mind; I didn't have to explain my thoughts. "It seems like a lifetime, but really, I married a man I met a few months ago."

He pulled me on top of him, my hair falling beneath my chin. "You married a man that loves you and we actually met the day after you were born. We just lost touch for a while in the middle."

I traced his lips. "You're so handsome," I said, staring into his eyes. Their color, of sea glass, reminded me of the happiest times of my messed-up childhood.

He rolled me to my side, propping his head up with his right arm. "How did I get so lucky?" he said, his fingers gliding down my ribs toward my hip bone.

"Like East said on the day we came here, luck had nothing to do with it."

He ran his finger up my body, and I shivered as he pulled a strand of hair behind my ear. "Do you believe that?" he asked.

I wrapped my right arm around his waist and pulled myself to him. "I do," I whispered.

His lips touched mine as softly as they could and still be felt. "I can't begin to tell you how much I love you," he said.

I returned the kiss with the same gentleness. "Then show me," I said, a smile filling my eyes as I lay my head against the pillow.

He followed, his lips not leaving mine. "Happily," he said, "for the rest of my life."

***

"How long can we stay here?" I asked as he cooked me breakfast on our second day of marriage.

The eggs sizzled against the cast iron. Jonah lifted the pan from the flame, careful not to touch the metal with his hand. "I was thinking we could make this our own, at least until wintertime."

"Is it safe?" I asked, eyeing the pistol that sat on top of our bags.

"I think it is, today," he said, handing me a plate of scrambled eggs and blackberries. "The future is hard to predict."

I chuckled. "The future was always hard to predict. We just didn't realize it."

"I'm a smart man for marrying such a smart woman," he said, and leaned over the table to kiss me. "Do you mind if I say a blessing before we eat?"

"You always say a blessing before you eat," I answered, aware that when he sat with his eyes closed with food in front of him, he was praying, and he did this before every meal.

"I'd like to say it out loud. But if it makes you uncomfortable, I won't."

For the briefest of thoughts I wanted to say no, keep your prayers to yourself, but realized I wanted all of him, not part of him. His faith was a big part of who he was, and I loved who he was. "I want you to be you," I said.

I lowered my head, out of respect, as he crossed himself and said thank-you for our food and for our life together.

"Have you always done that?" I asked as we ate.

"Said a prayer before I eat?"

I nodded.

"No." He shook his head. "My mom always did it when I was little, but when I didn't eat with her I didn't do it. Even when I did eat with her, I was usually halfway done before she sat down, so I guess I got only half my food blessed," he joked.

"When did you start?"

He swallowed and took a sip of water. "When I was in jail—that's when everything started. I'm sure you must see me as very devout, but for most of my life I was lukewarm, at best. If there was a chance to miss Mass, I would take it. Now—"

"Now you run into abandoned churches in hopes of finding the Eucharist," I said before biting into a blackberry.

He nodded. "It hurts me that I took it for granted for so long. That I didn't care and didn't believe—not really."

"I'm sure God has forgiven you."

He smiled weakly. "Yeah, he has, but it still hurts. That probably doesn't make sense to you."

I lowered my gaze and thought of the things I wished I'd done differently. The things God would, or maybe already had forgiven, but which still—if I let them—would control me.

I rolled a blackberry between my fingers. "I think we have to accept our pasts. We have to forgive ourselves and each other. Sometimes you speak of the evil one—which, by the way, when you do that, does sound a little crazy." I smiled. "But I think if there is a sort of brain behind evil, keeping us tied to our past mistakes would be the best way to keep us from moving forward."

He took my hand in his. "I have spent hundreds, if not thousands of hours in prayer, and still you have a purity and a wisdom I can only hope to one day be given."

I laughed. "I can assure you I am neither pure nor wise."

"You are wise, quite wise, and when I say purity, I mean purity of intention. You are good, even if your actions didn't always match up." He raised his eyebrows in a teasing way.

I giggled at his silly face, popping the last blackberry into my mouth.

"Are you ready to visit the others?" he asked, picking up his empty plate.

"We're coming back here tonight, right?" I asked, not willing to sacrifice my time alone with him. I stood and stretched.

"Oh, trust me," he said, putting the plate back on the table and standing. He wrapped an arm around my waist and pulled me to him. "We will definitely be here tonight."

I giggled as his lips tickled my neck. I swung around, wrapping my arms around him as we fell onto the bed.

Twenty-Six
EAST

A few electric lights shone through the windows, creating an unnatural glow. Guns fired in the distance. The sound was monotonous. I shouldn't think that way about guns. People were probably dying, but after hours of continuous fire, the sound blended into nothingness.

Eight sets of eyes watched us, some more closely than others. The girl with the long braid, Amber, was clearly one of the leaders. She was also one of the older ones. I guessed she was fifteen or sixteen. Her red hair and skin dotted with freckles made her stand out. She continued to watch us closely. The two boys, Xander and Harley, were completely comfortable around us and the rest of their group followed their lead. They were wrong to be so relaxed; we were strangers and we could be enemies.

"How did all of you come to be together?" John asked, faint shadows playing across his face from the outside lights.

"Most of us have been together for years," Harley said. "Nevaeh was the last to join us and that was more than a year ago." He pointed to a girl no older than Juliette, whose black hair was tightly braided against her scalp.

Haz asked him, "Where were you before?"

I doubted they were from the same family; they had different shades of skin and hair and they were all only three or four years apart in age. Even the most spirit-filled families in our parish weren't open to adopting eight kids so close in age.

"Foster care," Harley said.

"We lived in a group home," Xander added.

I immediately thought of Jael and Ash, and of the gift of family Momma Pryce had given them.

"Why are you wearing slave clothes?" Haz asked, his tone solemn.

"Slave clothes?" John asked, appalled.

"They rounded us up right after the attack," Xander said, ignoring John's reaction.

"Rounded you up?" Haz raised an eyebrow.

Harley said, "They were nice at first."

Amber snorted in disapproval.

"Okay, not nice, but they gave us food," Harley said.

"Yeah," Amber said, "and made us slaves."

John stared at these freedom fighters, but said nothing.

"Are you slaves?" I asked.

"Obviously not," Amber responded. "We wouldn't be here if we were slaves."

"But you were?" I said, trying not to respond to her tone that was clearly meant to tell me how stupid I was.

"For like, a minute," Xander said.

"Did they let you go?" John asked.

Xander snickered. "You might say that."

"They had no idea what they were getting themselves into, did they?" Haz asked, with a smile that showed off his dimples.

"Not a clue," Amber said, smirking.

"The thing about foster care is you either learn not to allow others to define you or you crumble, and none of us crumbled," Xander said proudly.

"They couldn't control you," Haz said with a hint of amusement.

"Not so much," Amber said, allowing herself to relax a little.

Harley said, "It turned out we weren't good at being servants, so we left."

I asked, "If you left, why are you still wearing slave clothes?"

"Are you kidding? These are the best things ever," Xander said. "They're like a free pass to go anywhere and request anything we want. All we have to do is pretend to be depressed and beaten down, and they think we're actually slaves."

"Smart," Haz said, nodding. "Is that how you find food?"

The pile of empty cans in the corner of the hallway indicated they weren't hunting.

"Mostly," Harley said, "but we're good at getting what we need in a variety of ways." His eyes twinkled in a mischievous way.

"I'm sorry, I'm confused. You all," John said, gesturing to the freedom fighters, "were *actual* slaves and there are others who are *actual* slaves?"

The freedom fighters glanced at one another.

"Yes," Amber replied, "we were *actual* slaves, and yes, there are lots more *actual* slaves."

"We've tried to help some of them escape," Xander said, "but their minds have been warped."

"They're terrified," Nevaeh said defiantly from the back of the group.

"They are terrified," Amber agreed.

"But you weren't terrified?" John asked, trying to understand what made these children so different from so many other people.

"We got out fast," Harley said.

Xander said, "It's more than that, that sets us apart."

Amber straightened her back. "When the people who're supposed to protect you when you're a little kid are the ones who hurt you, that changes you," she said, her voice hard and emotionless.

"Stuff affects us differently," Xander said in a softer tone. "We aren't like other people. I used to think that was bad, like it was a burden that we had to carry. The truth is, it was preparing us to survive in this world."

"Turns out we're the lucky ones," Harley said.

"Who knew," another boy joked.

They all laughed, but a sort of sad silence followed their laughter.

"What about you?" Xander asked after a few seconds. "What's your story?"

I pulled at a fray from the worn carpet.

Haz pushed his injured leg in front of his body. "You mean, who were we before the EMPs?" he asked.

They nodded.

"I was a DC cop," Haz answered.

They shifted in their positions, some cutting glances at others.

Haz continued, ignoring their discomfort. "I met East a few months ago in the city. We escaped the city. Eventually, we met John."

"Actually, they rescued me," he said.

Amber sat forward. "Rescued you from where?" she asked.

"I was being held at Camp David," John answered.

"The president's vacation place?" Harley asked.

"It wasn't much of a vacation, but yes, that's the place," he answered.

"Are you, like, the president or something?" Harley asked.

"No," John said, shaking his head. "I was a senator." His voice had an edge of embarrassment to it.

Xander said, "They rescued you, and you all decided to come back here?"

"Why?" Amber asked, skepticism returning to her voice.

John coughed and said, "To find my family."

"And to understand what was happening here," I added. There was no reason to allow John to blame our presence here entirely on himself.

"You risked your life coming into a war zone, to find your family?" Amber asked, with confusion.

I understood how right Amber was: when the people who are supposed to love you are the ones who hurt you, it changes you.

"Yes," John answered. I could sense his sadness for the kids who sat in front of him.

Amber gazed at him and said, "What did they look like? What part of the city were they in? Maybe we've seen them, or if not, then we can help you find them."

She appreciated that he loved his family. It was a love she had not had, yet one that she valued.

"Thank you," John said, staring into her eyes with an expression of deep appreciation.

He cleared his throat. "We lived south of the city, across the Potomac. My wife, Camille, is the smartest, kindest, most beautiful woman I've ever met. We have two kids. Our boy Johnny is sixteen and is very special. Some people would say he has disabilities. We disagree, but he is noticeably different from others his age. Our girl, Juliette, is twelve. She's an extraordinary young woman and other than my wife, she's my best friend. My son can't understand a lot of things, but she can. She can understand everything." His eyes began to turn red. "She's always understood everything." He sniffed the tears back. "It made life difficult for her. Too much for her. She isn't like all of you. There was a lot she couldn't handle. Life often overwhelmed her and made her silent."

Haz's eyes moved to mine.

"My wife homeschooled her. Juliette was so happy in the silence. It didn't matter that Camille didn't actually want to homeschool the kids. It's what she thought was best for the kids, so that's what she did." John's voice broke at the memory.

"They sound lovely," Amber said kindly.

John nodded once, his eyes tearful.

"Does your daughter have your eyes?" I asked, seeing in my mind the silent young girl staring back at me.

With hesitation, John said, "Yes."

Haz leaned his back against the wall of the building and ran his fingers over his head, rubbing his scalp.

"What is it?" John asked, watching us watch each other.

"We know where your daughter is," Haz said.

"Where?" John said, his voice anxious.

His eyes settled on me. "North Carolina," I answered.

Twenty-Seven
BRIA

"Ah, the newlyweds," Eli said as we approached him on the path that connected the main house to my parents' old house. "Something's different about you two. You have a sort of glow to your complexions." Eli winked, and I felt myself blush.

"Cut it out, you're a priest," Jonah said, dismounting from Fulton. He offered me his hand, and I accepted it and slid off Talin.

"I was your brother long before I was a priest," Eli said to Jonah. "I'm happy for you both. Welcome to the family, Bria. We're blessed to have you," he said, giving me a gentle hug.

"The feeling is mutual," I said.

"Where're you going?" Jonah asked.

"To Bria's old house. Holt said Heath and Maria should use it. We were running out of space in the main house, and Holt said it was sitting empty and he didn't want to live there. He didn't think you'd want to, either," he said, looking at me.

I shook my head, staring at the ground. I still wasn't ready to return to my childhood home.

"That's what he figured, so Heath and Maria are going to use it."

Jonah said, "And you're going to visit?"

"No, Isabelle wasn't feeling well yesterday, after they got all moved in. Felicia sent me with some herbs for her, and I thought I'd say a healing blessing."

"Does that work?" I asked.

"It certainly can, though I'm a fan of modern medicine. But Nonie told me to say a blessing and I don't disobey my grandmother."

"Do you want to take Fulton?" Jonah asked.

"You don't mind?" Eli said.

"No, here." Jonah gave him the reins.

I held the container of herbs Felicia had prepared and his book of prayers, and handed them up to Eli.

"Tell them we hope she feels better," I said.

"I'll tell them you will be praying. You have to put some power behind your hope," he said as he rode away.

"Is he going to try to convert me too?" I asked, shaking my head as we made our way on foot up to the house. Holding the loose reins with my left hand, I led Talin.

"I don't think so. That's not his style," Jonah said. "He believes God brings people to the church when it's their time to enter it."

"That sounds like a good way to avoid responsibility," I said.

Jonah took my free hand. "It is a fine line between wanting to share the most amazing experience you've ever had with someone, while still respecting their own beliefs or lack of beliefs," he said.

His grip tightened for half a second and then he loosened his fingers around mine. I understood he was walking that line with me. Though he wanted to share more, he was being patient and respecting where I was. I was grateful for that.

From the back of the house, we could hear voices, especially JP's and Quinn's, who were yelling about something.

"They argue so much," Jonah said. "It reminds me of how East and I were as kids." He squeezed my hand at the mention of her name.

We were spotted as soon as we came around the corner. Children and adults rushed to us to give us hugs. Sara and Blaise wanted details—I could see it in their eyes—and Josh hit Jonah on the back harder than he'd intended. Our parents were respectful, loving, and welcoming. JP, Quinn, and Juliette were happy we were back. Juliette squeezed me tight.

"I never told you how fantastic your playing was at the wedding," I said as she let me go.

"Did you like it?" she asked with excitement.

"It was incredible," I said.

"I've been working on a new song," she said. "I'll play it for your later."

"One you composed?" I asked.

She shook her head. "I'm still trying to learn the basics of violin."

"You have more than the basics," Charlotte said. "She's better than anyone I've ever heard before."

"A prodigy," Richard said.

"Thank you," Juliette said bashfully.

I could tell that was not the first time she had been called a prodigy. The curiosity of her past life overwhelmed me at times. I wanted to know, but didn't want to ask. Her telling me meant she'd be forced to think of the people she loved, who were no longer with her.

Sara and Blaise took my hand. "Come on, we need your help with something in the orchard," Blaise said as they pulled me forward.

Jonah took Talin's reins from me and smiled in amusement.

"How was it? Tell us everything!" Blaise blurted when we were away from the others.

"Oh, not everything," Sara said, wincing in pretend disgust.

"It was a good night," I said.

"You've been gone two and a half days," Blaise said, blinking at me.

I laughed. "I guess time got away from us."

"Was it amazing? I totally bet it was amazing," Blaise said.

"It was …"—I paused—"everything it should be." I realized that was the difference I felt with Jonah. When we were together physically, yes, it was beyond anything I could have imagined and yes, I loved him more than I ever thought possible. But it was more than that. It was, in fact, the fulfillment of a promise—a promise in which we gave our whole selves to each other. Neither of us was holding back. We were free in the fullest sense of the word and that freedom brought with it a level of pleasure I never would have dreamed possible.

"You seem different," Sara said, "and not just in a 'you had good sex' kinda way."

The laugh was out before I could stop it. "No, that's not the difference, though it was incredible," I said with a sly smile.

"Oh, I knew it would be," Blaise said, clasping her hands and twirling as if she were the princess in a fairy tale. "I mean, Jonah is *so* Jonah, and you, you had such a winding road. But you made it. Oh, I am so happy for you!" She hugged me.

I glanced at Sara, silently asking if I should be offended. Sara shook her head at Blaise.

"We simply need to find a man for Sara and we will be all set," Blaise said.

I raised my eyebrows.

"I told you I'm good," Sara said patiently.

"You said that, but how can you be?" Blaise asked.

"Honestly, I'm pretty sure I met my lifetime man quota by the time I was eighteen. The last few years were way unnecessary," she said with remorseful amusement.

"But don't you see? If Bria can find her true love, you can too!" Blaise said emphatically.

I realized they had had this conversation before.

"I'm open to what the Lord is calling me to, but I don't think it's marriage," Sara said.

"That's ridiculous," Blaise said. "Marriage is wonderful. Why wouldn't you want to get married?"

"Marriage is wonderful," Sara said, "and if God wants me to get married he will make that clear. Though, I think he's calling me more to himself."

"Ugh, I swear," Blaise said in frustration. "Your conversion to Catholicism was a bad idea. No one in my home church or Josh's ever talked like that. People practiced chastity, for sure, but not celibacy. You can love the Lord and give him your life and still be married."

"That is definitely true," Sara said, staying calm when Blaise was not.

That in itself was odd; however, this whole conversation was odd.

Sara was saying, "If marriage is the vocation God is inviting you to. But it is equally true that God sometimes invites us to the consecrated life, and we must have the courage to say yes to that vocation as well."

"Bizarre!" Blaise said. "The Catholic view on that whole area is bizarre!"

"What area?" I asked.

"She's talking about being a nun," Blaise said in exasperation.

"A nun?" I asked.

"That's not true," Sara said. "I have not discerned if God is calling me to be a nun or a religious sister or a consecrated single. Not that the nuances matter all that much at this point, since it's not like I can pick out a religious order and go join it."

I focused intently on the apple tree beside me, instead of my friends. My face showed total confusion and I was afraid the confusion would be interpreted as disagreement with one person and agreement with the other. The truth was I didn't understand enough of what they were saying to disagree or agree.

But Blaise clearly understood and completely disagreed. She quoted the Bible, and then Sara quoted a different part of the Bible, and while I listened and tried to comprehend, I didn't. Their words sounded like gibberish.

I slowly stepped away until I was able to turn, unnoticed, and go back toward the house. The two of them were lost in a debate that was nuanced and confusing, and not all that interesting.

***

"Where have you been?" Jonah said, kissing me softly when I returned to his side.

"Blaise and Sara wanted details," I said, raising and lowering my eyebrows.

"What'd you say?" he asked.

"Oh, you know, that it was decent." I smirked.

"Decent?" he said, shocked. "I mean, I have nothing to compare it to, but if that is decent, I am seriously happy to be married."

"I'm teasing. I told them it was everything it should've been, and I think I understand that now too."

"You do?"

"Yeah, the whole covenant thing and giving your whole self, holding nothing back. It sounded weird when Eli explained it before we got married, but now that we're actually living it, I totally get it."

He took my hand in his and ushered me toward the house. "I agree. I understood it intellectually before, but now I feel it. Like you *are* mine and I *am* yours and we are one, but two, at the same time. It's extraordinary," he said, bending forward to kiss me as we walked.

"Eli's back," JP called from around the corner of the house.

A second later Eli and Fulton came into view. He rode to the barn and we followed to make sure Fulton and Talin were taken care of.

"How's Isabelle?" Jonah asked.

"Sick, but not too sick," Eli said. "Felicia's concoction seemed to help quite a bit, even in the short time I was there. Her knowledge of herbal remedies is a godsend."

Inside me, emotion started to swirl.

We put up the horses and left the barn with Eli. Felicia, Nonie, and Charlotte came toward us.

"How is she?" Nonie asked.

"Better. Felicia's remedy seemed to help," Eli said.

"Praise God," Felicia said, clapping her hands.

Again, the emotion swirled. I could not name it, but the feel of it made me want to scream.

The three of them went in the direction of the garden, chatting and laughing.

"I didn't realize they were such good friends," I said as we watched them go. This time I could name the feeling—dread.

"Richard and Felicia have fit in nicely," Eli said. "And they're hard workers. Richard has already begun working with Sara and Dad to design a windmill."

"A windmill?" Jonah asked.

"Sara says if we can salvage the right parts, we could create electricity," Eli answered.

"Really?" I asked.

"That's what she says, but even if we can't use it for electricity, we could use it as a mill to grind flour," he said.

"So much is going on here," I said, feeling oddly left out.

"You two have been a bit preoccupied," Eli said, and smiled.

It was true. Leading up to the wedding we spent a lot of time with him or with Charlotte and Quint or even Blaise and Josh, learning from them about the different aspects of marriage. We'd been almost exclusively focused on ourselves for the last few weeks. I felt selfish at this realization. In that time, friendships had been formed—friendships I wasn't entirely happy about—and the possibility of electricity, which I was happy about. I wondered what else I had missed.

That night at dinner I focused not on myself or Jonah, but on everyone else. Felicia and Richard had indeed been fully integrated into the group and that awareness brought another surge of discomfort. This time I understood it. They were murderers. Did the others know? Did they understand their new friends had killed a child and her parents and probably others before them?

When we brought Felicia and Richard with us, it never occurred to me that they would become friends with the people I loved. The memory of the murders made my stomach hurt and my head spin. I closed my eyes and saw the girl, Annalise, falling to the ground, her body becoming still and empty as the blood drained onto the white gravel. Were her parents still alive when she died? Was there still some awareness of this life as they slipped into the next? Did they watch their child die?

I set my bowl of rabbit stew down and left the fire and voices. I was sure Jonah was watching me, wondering where I was going. I didn't want to worry him or anyone else, but I couldn't stay there. I couldn't watch the killers share a meal with people I loved.

I heard the footsteps and I turned, expecting to see Jonah, but Eli was there.

"I hope you don't mind," he said. "I'm sure you'd prefer to talk to Jonah, but I thought a priest might be better for this one."

"What do you mean?" I asked.

"I saw you watching Felicia and Richard."

I leaned against the apple tree, my right arm around it. "Do you know what they did?" I asked. There would be no reason for him to be here if he didn't.

He nodded.

"How can you allow that?" I said, my voice quiet yet charged by anger.

"The others do too," he said, his hands in his pockets, the stance reminding me of Jonah.

My dinner threatened to leave my stomach. I gripped the tree with two hands, my face pressed against its rough bark. In the fading light of summer, I could see the tiny green apples growing on the branches.

"They told us, all of us, shortly after they arrived."

I wanted to ask why I hadn't been told any of this, but I already knew the answer. I'd been focused on myself for so long that I had forgotten about the rest of the world.

"Have you told JP?" My voice, like the rest of me, was in a state of disbelief.

"No. None of the kids are aware of their past."

"Except Juliette, because she saw them kill Annalise's family," I said in disgust.

"You're right, she's aware. And I guess technically she is a kid, but I never think of her like that. She has more wisdom and understanding than most adults."

He was right; she wasn't a kid, not really.

I inhaled and lifted my face from the tree. "So everyone is fine with them killing an innocent family and who knows how many people before that?" I said in a bitter voice.

"Six," Eli said.

I said nothing.

"They killed six others before the family you saw."

My nails gripped the tree as a surge of pain ran through my body. My hands released and I slumped onto the ground, my body leaning against the tree, one arm around it, its stability offering me some form of hope.

"How?" I breathed quick and shallow. "How can you let them be around JP and Quinn?" East flashed in my mind and the certain rage she would feel at Quinn being so close to heartless child-killers. She told me to protect her. I promised to protect her.

Eli sat in front of me, his legs crossed. "They're sorry."

"They're sorry!" I shouted with rage. "Sorry doesn't bring back the nine people they killed, people they killed not in self-defense, but with the callousness of only the worst of humanity."

"The world has changed," he said softly.

My mouth fell open. "What is wrong with you? You were the man I confessed to, the man I first told of my abortion. You held me while I cried over the killing of my child, my one child. And yet these people kill other people's fully-grown kids and we're supposed to be fine with that? And forgive them?"

"Were you not forgiven?"

I wanted to scream. Instead, I said, "I was a kid. I was scared and alone and I was sorry. Sorry for years. Plagued by regret and pain for years."

"You're right, it doesn't seem fair. They were adults who knew what they were doing, but in a world that has lost all sense of objective truth."

"We didn't! We didn't lose it," I countered.

"You're right, we didn't. But I understand how others who never truly had it did. If you are simply living life, trying to be a good person, with no clear definition of what that means, your definition changes with society. Our society changed, Bria. Overnight, what was disgusting—killing and eating a dog—became a means of survival."

"A dog is not a human."

"No, and we recognize the objective distinction between the two and the objective difference in the value of the life of a human from the life of a dog, but others don't, and I guess, Bria, I get it. You're good, you truly are,"—he held up a hand to stop my interruption—"and so for you, yes, you had an abortion, and soon after, you understood—without anyone explaining things to you—that you had killed, even when others said you hadn't."

"I felt it," I said, remembering. "I felt my child's life end within me. For a while I thought I was imagining it, that my guilt had created some weird sensation, but I had no guilt until that moment, when I felt my baby's life slip away."

"See, that's what I mean. Most people don't have that. That sets you apart and it makes you feel the injustice and the pain of this situation more than what others might feel."

I wanted to roll my eyes, but didn't. "They … are … murderers," I said, my jaw set tight.

"They didn't have to tell us," he said softly.

"Ohhh, give them a gold star!" I said sarcastically. "Who cares that they told you."

"Don't you see? They confessed their sins to all of us. They were honest. They weren't forced to do it. No one had told on them, but they chose to face the truth rather than bury it with more lies."

"I don't care," I said.

"They built memorials."

I raised my head.

"In the cemetery, they built nine grave markers and chiseled the names of their victims onto the stones. I sat with them as they did it," he said solemnly.

My heart turned.

"The tears, the pain they felt for the deaths they had caused was intense,"—again he held up a hand, stopping my words—"and warranted. Bria, God has forgiven them. He was the first to forgive them. The rest of us also have to."

"What about Blaise?" I asked, realizing that even at dinner she'd kept her distance from them.

"She's trying, and she is moving forward. It helped her when they were honest, and it helped her to see the memorials they built. In some ways, she has taken their sin as her own, and she's working through that. She has to learn to accept that though they are her parents, the state of their soul is not hers."

"So I should forget what I saw?" I asked, feeling pain replace anger.

"No, we never forget. You, of all people, realize that. But we do move forward slowly, rebuilding trust."

I made a face of disbelief.

"Bria, if things were different, if they hadn't been honest and we somehow found out, or if they carried on with their lives as if nothing had happened, it would be difficult to forgive. Still, we would be called to do it, for our own sake, if not for theirs. But it would have been a lot harder. And in that case, it would not be about rebuilding trust. In fact, I would have suggested that they leave. You're right. Having them here without their understanding of the gravity of their sin would have been impossible and potentially dangerous.

"Thankfully, that is not where we are. Thankfully, they are intensely sorry and are taking full responsibility for their actions. I'm fairly certain that if you all had not destroyed that camp in your escape, they would have already left here to do so. The Lord uses the least of his children to do great things. It's not up to us to figure out how he is going to use them, but they have opened themselves up to him and, to be honest, it's beautiful to witness."

"Is Jonah aware of all this?"

Eli nodded. "I told him one day while I was helping him build your honeymoon suite."

"I wonder why he didn't tell me," I said, feeling betrayed.

"He had a hard time with it as well. As much as I mess with him, his heart is so pure, like yours, that to accept murder ... it must be almost impossible. If either of you truly comes to forgive and accept them, it will be a grace from God.

"But I think, ultimately, he didn't tell you because he didn't want you to have to deal with any of that before your wedding. He wanted you focused on him, like he was focused on you. When you left dinner, he let me come to you. He understood it was time for you to be told what was going on and probably that you might be upset with him for not telling you."

My anger at Jonah dissipated; he was trying to protect me. I would have done the same for him. Though, we should be more honest in the future and not worry about protecting each other. I wanted to go to him, to tell him that from now on we'd go through stuff together and not keep secrets.

Eli stood and offered me his hand. "Let's go back. You left half a bowl of stew, and even Jonah will only be able to protect that for so long ... until JP figures out a way to make it his."

I forced a weak smile. I was glad Jonah and I would be alone tonight.

Twenty-Eight
EAST

"North Carolina?" John repeated.

"It's where I'm from and where my brother and friends were going back to," I answered.

"How?" John stared at me.

"Juliette found us," Haz said solemnly. "And she saved us. She showed us how to leave the city. The south is not like here. There, there's a wall and a river. It was a difficult area to escape, but she showed us the way."

John said, "She just walked up to you and showed you how to escape the city?"

Haz looked at me as if wondering how much to disclose.

I lifted my head to the heavens and prayed for guidance. "She was a"—I forced out the word—"slave."

John's face turned to one of fear and stone.

I said, "In a building run by the government. We went there with someone one of us knew. He wasn't good, and we were ambushed. One of us, Bria, was left behind. We tried to save her." I swallowed hard. "But we couldn't. She was captured and we couldn't get to her. Juliette's actions saved Bria's life then … and later."

It had always been obvious to me that it was Juliette, not Bria, who forced the knife into his throat, saving Bria's life and ending Trent's.

"Your daughter is very brave. She saved all of us," Haz added.

"A slave," John said, stumbling over the words. "What did she—what was her job?" he said, his face drained of color.

The assembled fighters who wore slave clothes looked away or down, but they didn't look at me and they certainly didn't look at John.

"She never told us," I said, thankful for Juliette's silence.

"What about her mom and brother? Were they ..." John's voice faltered.

Haz rubbed his injured leg. "She didn't speak about them, either," he said.

"She never said if they were alive?" John asked, desperate to learn what happened to his family.

I shook my head.

He stared, not understanding how there was so much we didn't know.

"John, you said before that there were times when Juliette stopped speaking." I lifted my eyes to his. "And that was before this world," I said, trying to help him understand.

John's expression fell.

"By the time we left her, she was speaking," Haz said.

Haz's words were true. There had been only a few words, but it showed she was healing.

John lowered his head into his hands and wept. There was much to cry for. I lifted my eyes upward. The white squares of ceiling tiles created a grid pattern. I prayed for John to be given strength, and for Juliette and all those she was with to be given peace.

In the darkened silence, the freedom fighters silently slipped away to different parts of the building. Xander and another boy stood near windows on either side of the building. They watched the shadows below us. Another, Nevaeh, sat near the stairs. These three were on guard. The others curled up in different offices, some on couches, others in chairs.

***

The shooting began again, this time louder and more frequent. Haz stood. I followed him. John remained, staring into nothingness, like he'd been doing for the last hour.

"Both sides are well armed," Xander said. "They can go on like this all night."

Haz and I watched. Occasionally we could see a splash of exploding light in the distance.

"Snipers?" I asked.

Xander nodded. "On both sides."

"You should sleep," Xander said to us. "We've got this."

He was right on both counts. I turned and Haz followed. We felt safe here. I returned to my spot on the floor, beside John.

"I'm leaving you in the morning," John said after a few more minutes of listening to the shooting.

"Where are you going?" I asked, already sure of the answer.

"North Carolina," he said with an edge of defiance.

"You won't make it," Haz said bluntly.

"I'll die trying."

"That would be a waste," I said. "I'll take you there, but not yet."

John shook his head. "No, I leave tomorrow."

"You think you're leaving for your daughter's sake, but you aren't," Haz said, keeping his voice low. "Juliette's safe. She's well protected and she's loved. She doesn't need you getting yourself killed on a foolish whim of selfish love."

"Do you have a child?"

Haz slowly shook his head.

"Then you have no idea what love is," John responded.

"I do," I said softly, aware of Haz's surprised eyes staring at me. "I do have a child, and I love her enough to accept that what she needs is not my physical presence, but a world that will allow her to live. I will take you to Juliette—

you have my word. But first we need to finish what we came here to do."

John leaned forward in anger. "We came to search for my family. We will not find Juliette here, and she will be able to tell me where her mother and brother are."

"We also came to learn," Haz said, "so that knowledge can be used to help us and the others make this country safe for both of your children."

"How long?" John said, grudgingly.

"A few more days in the city," I said.

He appeared hopeful.

"And then we go to Raven Rock and tell Jael and Ash what we've learned," Haz said, completing my thoughts.

"No, that's too long," John said, shaking his head in anger.

"After Raven Rock, we'll both take you to Juliette," Haz said.

"What about the war?" I asked, surprised by Haz's offer to go with us.

"Something tells me the war will still be here when I get back," he said with resolve. "Besides, I miss Juliette and I'd like to meet your daughter, East."

He was a good man. That was clear to me as soon as I met him. This only confirmed how good of a man he truly was.

"We leave from Raven Rock," John said. "We don't take a detour back to the town."

That meant we would not see Momma Pryce or Becca or the others again for a long time.

"We will leave from Raven Rock," Haz said, extending his hand to John.

"From Raven Rock," John said as they clasped hands, staring into each other's eyes.

This promise would not be broken.

Twenty-Nine
BRIA

"You don't like it, do you?" Sara asked as we scraped the hide of a doe, using sharpened bones to separate the fat from the skin.

She could tell I wasn't thinking of the task at hand; my mind was elsewhere and my eyes were watching JP and Richard weed the garden.

I swallowed and shook my head.

"You don't trust them," she said.

"Should I?" I asked, reluctantly turning my attention to her.

"Maybe," she said, watching the man and the boy.

"That's not reassuring," I scoffed.

"It wasn't meant to be," she said. "What they did was so … so …"

"Horrific, disgusting, heinous," I said.

"Yes, all of those," she said. "But they have said they're sorry."

"Do you think that matters to the nine people they killed and those that still mourn them? Do you think they care that the people that killed them said sorry?"

"What else can they do?" she asked.

"Nothing," I acknowledged. "There's nothing they can do to bring back the people they killed."

I pulled a layer of fat from the skin. Franklin snatched it from me before I could dump it into the bucket. Nonie would be mad at the dog for that, but I wouldn't tell.

"I don't think we can hate them forever," Sara said softly.

"I don't hate them," I said, "but I don't trust them and I don't plan to. I'm not okay with them being alone with the kids and I'm not okay with them having weapons."

"You think they're going to hurt us?" she asked skeptically.

"Why wouldn't they?"

"Bria, what they did before—"

"Killed, what they did before was kill," I said, angry at her attempt to downplay the severity of their actions.

"It was because of where they were," she said. "Murdering was normal in the harvesters' camp. Life wasn't respected there. It is respected here and murdering is not allowed."

"So they will murder if it's allowed?" I asked.

"The truth is most people rely on authority to tell them how to live, and when that authority changes, the way they live changes," Sara said sadly. "But I think they've learned their lesson. They've realized they need to base their lives on a different authority. They understand they have to live differently than the rest of the world, or they will be as awful as the rest of the world."

"Great," I said. "They were good because the world said that's how they should be. Then the world said they should be evil, so they became evil. Now they are trying to be good again, or maybe they actually are good again. But for how long? If they leave here and are surrounded by evil, will they be evil again?"

JP looked up from his work in the garden row closest to us and saw me watching him. He waved and I waved in return. Richard smiled, stretched, and returned to the weeding.

Sara said, "I suppose there's no way to know that."

"How is Blaise doing with all of this?" I asked. I didn't have the courage to ask her directly.

"She puts on a good act, but it's been beyond awful for her," Sara said as she stripped the last layer of fat from the hide. "Eli and I have given her biblical examples and even some saints who have committed horrific acts and then allowed God in their life in a powerful way. That has helped her. Her faith is strong and she is praying for the grace to forgive. She will get there eventually, and her family will be healed. I have to believe that."

"You're right," I said. "She will forgive them. I believe that." And once she forgave them, I probably would too. Part of my anger at them was on her behalf. After she was healed, my anger would fade. Though that didn't mean I would trust them.

We turned the hide and began scraping away the hair.

"Do you really want to be a nun?" I asked, remembering what Blaise and Sara had been arguing about before.

Sara's face was transformed into one of serene happiness. "I do, I really do," she said, her voice almost giddy.

"That means no guys ever," I said, thinking back over my short marriage and not understanding how she could choose to not have a husband. If she never met anyone worthy of her, that would be one thing. But to actively say no to all of them? That was something entirely different.

"And I'm completely okay with that," she said.

"You haven't met the right guy," I said.

"That's just it. I have met *the* right guy." She sighed. "He happens to be the second person of the Trinity."

"You mean Jesus?" I asked, deciphering what she meant.

"I do," she said.

I scraped my blade of sharpened bone down the skin, pulling with it a thick clump of hair. "Don't you think he'd want you to have an actual man to share your life with?" I asked.

"That is what he wanted for *you*, but no, I don't believe that's what he wants for me."

I didn't understand this, but I didn't have to. I could tell by her far-off, dreamy expression that she was in love, as much, if not more than I was. And she was happy, happier than I had ever seen her. For these reasons, I was happy for her and in the end it didn't matter if I understood or not.

After several more passes with the bone scraper, the hide was free of hair.

"I'm happy for you, Sara."

"Thank you, Bria." Her smile was wide and full of love.

Thirty
BRIA

"How was your day?" Jonah asked as he stood before me in our one-room home, a luxury retreat that we would keep until the snow began to fall and the nights were too cold to stay here.

We spent most of our days away from one another. He and Eli roamed the woods for hours at a time. They searched for game trails—though that was primarily left to Josh and Blaise—and trees that were diseased and, thus, good for fuel, and straight trees good for building. Jonah and Eli worked as a team, chopping the trees and carrying them out. They were our forest managers, ensuring we took from nature in a sustainable way.

I sat at our table and sipped warm lavender tea. "Sara and I stripped the hair off three hides and soaked them in brain solution. They should be ready to be stretched and softened tomorrow or the next day," I said.

"That's great," he said. "We need the leather."

"We always need the leather," I joked.

With this many adults and growing children, leather was always in short supply.

"We checked some of the traps today," he said excitedly. "Juliette and Sage caught two rabbits."

"Were they alive?" I asked, feeling hopeful.

"They were," he said, sitting across from me. "Quinn and Isabelle have already named them."

"That's fine," I said. "They can name the adults, as long as they don't name the babies that are going to feed us this winter."

"Unfortunately, we now have four females, but we'll check the other traps tomorrow. We're sure to catch a male eventually," he said.

"That was a good idea Richard had, about catching rabbits to breed," I said.

"It was," Jonah said. "Between the rabbits and hogs and eggs, winter should be tolerable."

"Much more than it was last year when we were eating tree bark to stay alive," I said, shuddering at the memory.

"What about the alarm system?" I asked. "How is that working?"

"We have the whole perimeter enclosed. The challenge is making sure Astrea and Franklin hear it."

"Or their future puppies," I said, excited that we would have snuggly puppies to play with in a little over a month.

"Yes, or their puppies," he said, his eyes on mine, making my heart race.

"Things are coming together pretty well," I said as I poured him some tea.

The sun had set and a small fire burned in the fire pit beside us. When that was out, our light would be a candle made of deer fat—one of Felicia's contributions. She said we could use bayberries in the fall and they wouldn't smell as bad, but we used what we had and we had plenty of animal fat.

"They are," Jonah said, his gaze shifting to somewhere far away.

"What's wrong?" I asked.

"What makes you think something's wrong?" He shifted his focus back to me.

"We've been married almost two whole weeks," I teased. "I know your expressions."

He rubbed his hand against the ceramic mug that sat in front of him. "I was thinking about East."

I lowered my gaze and picked at a splinter on the table.

Thinking of East was always difficult. When she came into my mind I tried to push her from it. It was too difficult to reconcile my comfort and safety with the life she was living, one that probably involved no comfort or safety.

"I try not to think of her," I said, immediately wishing I hadn't been so honest.

He squeezed my hand. "I can't do that. Like she said, I've always tried to protect her. I've always failed, but I've always tried."

"You wanted to stay, didn't you?" I asked, the truth of the question filling me with pain.

"Yes," he said softly.

"But you didn't because of me." I stared at the table he and my father had made for us.

"Yes and no."

I felt some degree of relief, thankful he had not outrightly chosen me over his sister.

"We needed to find Blaise's parents and we needed to bring Juliette home. And Sara and Sage."

"But you regret it?" I asked.

"No, it was the right thing to do. It was the right decision and it allowed us to get married, and I will never for one second regret anything that led to our marriage," he said, squeezing my hands until I lifted my eyes to his.

"I'm sure she's safe," I said, lying.

"Remember, I can tell when you're lying," he said with a sad smile.

"I guess I'm not sure of it, but I do believe it," I said.

"I do too," he said. "Or at least East is alive. I feel her life. That probably sounds crazy."

"No, it doesn't," I said.

His expression was distant, and I could tell he had something more to say.

"What is it?" I asked. For some reason, fear welled inside me. This wasn't simply missing East. I felt something else, something that scared me.

He hesitated, and then said, "I feel like a coward for being here, safe and ridiculously happy, when she and Haz and the others are none of those things. They're literally risking their lives for us and our country, and we're doing nothing for them."

"What can we do?" I whispered, my voice shaking for some unexplained reason.

Moonlight illuminated the space the firelight did not. Jonah ran his fingers through his hair in a forceful way, as if trying to control his own rising anxiety.

He finally said, "I can't stay here."

"We can move to the main house," I said quickly.

He looked down and then up at me. "That's not what I meant."

My body shook. I wrapped my arms around my shoulders, trying to contain the fear that threatened to control me. My mind was shutting down as panic surged.

"I won't be gone long," he said, his voice low and sorry. "I'll check on her and come right back."

I laughed a ridiculous laugh that fit his ridiculous statement. "Have you lost your mind?" The words had come out mean and biting.

His back stiffened. I'd hurt him.

I stood and paced, trying to calm my body and mind.

After several minutes of my pacing and Jonah sitting with his head hung in defeat, he said, "I feel like a coward."

"But you aren't!" I said, louder than I'd meant to.

"I can tell when you're lying," he said sadly.

"I'm not lying! You're brave and strong and you're protecting your wife and your parents and all of your other siblings," I said, begging that he heard me.

"And none of you need protecting," he said. "This place would run fine without me. It's safe. So safe that the two of us can live away from the rest of the family and so can Heath and Maria. The area around here has been stable since before we left—we simply didn't know it. Trade has started. People aren't going out of their way to help others, but they aren't going out of their way to kill others, either. Meanwhile, East is in a war zone and I'm in a honeymoon suite. I can't do it, Bria. I can't be this much of a coward. That is not the man you fell in love with, it is not the man you married."

I wanted to break something, I wanted to scream, I wanted to cry. I didn't want him to see me. I rushed out of our house.

The night air was crisp, the stars bright, and the moon brighter.

He stepped beside me.

"How would you even find her?" I said, after my mind had calmed enough to allow words to form.

"I'll start at the town."

"What if she's not there? What if you go all that way, risking your life, and you can't find her?"

"I have to try," he said as if apologizing.

His hand reached to touch my shoulder. I wanted to give in to his touch, to allow my anger to calm. I pulled away, creating distance between us.

"You're being selfish," I said.

"I disagree."

The calmness of his voice added to my fury.

I turned to face him. "You are my husband and you're risking your life for nothing. You won't be able to find her, and, even if you can, what are you going to do? You said you're going to check on her and come right back. What's the point of that?"

"It's something I have to do," he said, refusing to back down.

I swallowed and said the only thing left to say. "I'm going with you."

In the light of the rising silver moon, I saw his face turn a ghostly white. He hadn't expected that. I felt victory. I had caused him pain, as he had caused me pain.

Tears came, and I turned away from him. I didn't want to cause him pain. I didn't want to hurt him even though he had hurt me.

His hands moved to my shoulders.

I sniffed. "I'm sorry. I said that to hurt you."

"It worked," he said, his voice filling with relief, and I understood that he thought I didn't mean what I had said.

"You know when I'm lying," I said softly.

Fear overtook him. It was all I could see and must have been all he could feel. I was sorry about that. Sorry that my speaking the truth had caused him pain.

"You're my husband. Our lives go together. 'And the two shall become one,' " I said, quoting the Bible.

"That's not what that means," he said.

"It's what it means to me. If you go, I go too."

He ran his fingers through his hair. "It's too dangerous."

"If it's safe enough for you, it's safe enough for me," I said, though in truth it wasn't safe for either of us.

"I can't risk your life," he said.

"But you can't stay here while East is out there. That's the rest of your thought, isn't it?"

He nodded.

"Jonah, I told you when we got married, that I wanted all of you and I meant it. I don't want you to become someone you aren't to appease me. If this is what you have to do, this is what you have to do. But I'm not a wife who's going to keep the home fires burning while her husband goes off to war. I'm not that strong."

We sat in silence, his face torn.

"Like you said, Jonah, we'll go and check on East, and come home. We'll be back before the first snowfall."

"Or we'll freeze to death," he said, lifting his gaze to mine.

I nodded and turned to go back into the home we shared. "Or we'll freeze to death together."

He followed. As we entered the room, I noticed the fire was almost out. He stopped me and held his arms out. My body sunk into his and we wrapped our arms around each other.

Our lives had intertwined. Some may not understand that, just as I didn't understand Jonah's need to search for

East. It made no sense, it was not logical … and neither was love. Not in its essence. Love was more than logic could explain. The love of a brother for his sister. The love of a wife for her husband. The love of a mother for her child. Love motivated East, and Jonah, and me to do things that were far from logical. It was this lack of logic, this love, that brought meaning to our world. Without it, we would have only pain.

End of Book Four

Also by Jacqueline Brown:

The Light: Who do you become when the world falls away?
Book One of The Light Series

Through the Ashes, Book Two of The Light Series

From the Shadows, Book Three of The Light Series

Out of the Darkness, Book Five of The Light Series

"Before the Silence," a Light Series short story

To receive your FREE copy of "Before the Silence," please visit Jacqueline-Brown.com

If you enjoyed *Into the Embers*, please consider sharing your copy with a friend and leaving a review.

www.ingramcontent.com/pod-product-compliance
Lightning Source LLC
Chambersburg PA
CBHW031219120726
47905CB00002B/391